Goddess Girls

CASSANDRA
THE
LUCKY

Goddess Girls

CASSANDRA
THE
LUCKY

JOAN HOLUB & SUZANNE WILLIAMS

Aladdin

NEW YORK   LONDON   TORONTO   SYDNEY   NEW DELHI

ALADDIN

An imprint of Simon & Schuster Children's Publishing Division

1230 Avenue of the Americas, New York, NY 10020

First Aladdin hardcover edition December 2013

Text copyright © 2013 by Joan Holub and Suzanne Williams

Jacket illustration copyright © 2013 by Glen Hanson

Also available in an Aladdin paperback cover edition.

For information about special discounts for bulk purchases, please contact
Simon & Schuster Special Sales at 1-866-506-1949 or business@simonandschuster.com.

The Simon & Schuster Speakers Bureau can bring authors to your live event. For more information or
to book an event, contact the Simon & Schuster Speakers Bureau at 1-866-248-3049
or visit our website at www.simonspeakers.com.

Designed by Karin Paprocki

The text of this book was set in Berthold Handcut Regular.

Manufactured in the United States of America 1113 FFG

2 4 6 8 10 9 7 5 3 1

Library of Congress Control Number 2013939120

ISBN 978-1-4424-8818-2 (hc)

ISBN 978-1-4424-8817-5 (pbk)

ISBN 978-1-4424-8819-9 (eBook)

CONTENTS

those words sometime in the next few days. Because Cassandra's prophecies always came true. Even if she was the only one who realized that fact!

"What are you doing?" demanded a concerned voice.

Cassandra had been concentrating so hard that she jerked her head up in surprise at the sudden question. She looked over to see her older sister, Laodice, coming into the bedroom the two girls shared.

The scent of peppermints and the vision both abruptly faded away. Of course, Laodice hadn't seen the vision. She'd be the first to admit that she couldn't prophesy her way out of a papyrus bag. Cassandra and her twin brother, Helenus, were the only ones in the family who could see the future.

And the fortunes they told—well, her brother's at least—went into the fortune cookies sold at their family's store. It was called the Oracle-O Bakery and was here in the Immortal Marketplace, which stood halfway between Earth and Mount Olympus.

Her mother had bought the store and this apartment right above it just two months ago. Even though Cassandra and her family were mortals, not immortals, they were fortunately allowed to live and own a shop in the IM.

"Nothing. I'm not doing anything," Cassandra told her sister. Quickly, before she could forget the words she'd foreseen, Athena would speak, she picked up a feather pen. After dipping the quill tip in a bottle of ink, she scribbled the words on a small piece of papyrus exactly one inch by four inches long. Then she set the fortune on a stack of others she'd already written.

Money was tight, and her family didn't have a lot of extra papyrus lying around. So she'd cut up an old drawing she'd done on the bakery letterhead stationery into these slips and written her fortunes on the backs of them.

"Are too. You're fortune-telling again," Laodice accused gently as she crossed the room.

Cassandra shrugged, her gaze flicking to the sundial on the windowsill. She'd been doing fortunes for almost an hour! Time always flew when she was having visions. She got into a mental zone, her own little world, where she didn't hear or see anything except the prophecies in her head. Prophecies no one ever believed, unfortunately, despite their truth. Instead she was widely considered to be a liar—and that really stung!

Laodice went over to the mirror that hung on the wall above her makeup table. As she passed Cassandra, the air stirred the golden moons, stars, and suns in the wind chimes dangling from the ceiling over Cassandra's desk. They clinked together merrily.

Every family that had a shop here in the Immortal Marketplace had a member with some special talent or magical ability, whether they were mortal or immortal. Helenus's much-praised prophetic talents were deemed sufficiently magical to qualify. Plus their family was *royalty*. Cassandra's mom was Queen Hecuba and her dad, King Priam of Troy. And that made Cassandra a Trojan princess!

She could see Laodice's reflection in the mirror as her sister brushed her long black hair and touched up her makeup. Her dark blue eyes went to the small stack of fortunes Cassandra had penned.

"I don't need to have visions to guess what you're up to," Laodice said. "And you'd better not let Mom catch you. You know you're not supposed to write prophecies anymore."

"I know," said Cassandra. "Don't tell, okay?"

"I won't," Laodice promised. "But you really should stop."

Cassandra glanced toward the door. "Where is Mom, anyway?"

"Minding the store," her sister informed her as she dusted some peach-colored face powder over her cheeks. "She wants us to come down and help at the counter selling cookies, because—"

Ka-boom!

At the sudden blast the two girls' eyes met, wide with fear. The noise had come from right below them. It had sounded and felt like an earthquake!

"What was that?" asked a rattled Cassandra. Had one of the cookie ovens malfunctioned and exploded or something? But Laodice was already out the door, heading downstairs. Hurriedly Cassandra stuffed the fortunes she'd written into the pocket of the lime-green chiton she was wearing and took off after her sister.

When they reached the store one floor below the

apartment, the two girls froze in their tracks. There was an enormous hole in the side wall of the shop—one as big as double doors. Clouds of smoke were billowing through it! No, wait, it wasn't smoke. It was dust!

"Oh," said Laodice, relaxing. "It's just the construction workers."

"Construction workers? What are construction workers doing here?" asked Cassandra.

Just then her mom breezed into the bakery through the hole. "They're knocking out a wall to join our store with the scrollbook shop next door," she explained.

"I only found out about the plan ten minutes ago myself," Laodice said to Cassandra. "Mom told me to tell you to expect some noise and dust, but when I got upstairs, I forgot. So it surprised me, too, when we heard that boom."

She'd forgotten? Typical! Laodice was really beautiful, but she could be an airhead. Ever since she'd turned fifteen, her brain had become pretty empty, unless you counted thoughts about *boys*.

Cassandra felt like pouting as she and her sister headed over to study the big hole in the wall. How could her mom have neglected to tell her that something this important might happen with the store? Nobody around here ever told her anything! It was like they all considered her a little kid. Hello? She was almost thirteen!

"But what happened to Mr. Euripides?" she wondered aloud as she peered through the cloud of dust into the scrollbook store. She pronounced his name: "yoo-RIP-uh-deez." He was the owner of the scrollbook store, and though all of his books were still there on the shelves like always, they were now a little dustier because of the construction.

"This very morning we struck a deal that's going to put our store on the map!" her mom enthused. She held up a contract in her hand that had her signature on it: *Hecuba of Troy*. "Lucky for us, he decided that the book business wasn't for him."

"He's gone off to live in a cave on an island somewhere," Laodice murmured to Cassandra. "Only decided this morning, then left immediately. I heard him tell Mom he's going to start a library there and concentrate on his writing."

"We're going to expand and combine the two stores," her mom went on. "Just as I've dreamed of. Isn't it fabulous?"

Cassandra nodded, though she felt torn. "Yeah, but it won't be the same around here without Mr. Euripides." It would be really fun to work in the scrollbook store however. She'd be able to read books whenever she wanted, as long as there were no customers. Still, she'd kind of miss Mr. Euripides. He was a great author. In fact, he'd won a famous Greek dramatic festival called the City Dionysia a total of five times! He'd told Cassandra she had great potential as a writer and had complimented her on the style of her dramatically written fortunes. Though even he didn't believe any of them actually came true.

"Maybe his retirement from the business was a good thing," Laodice remarked. "I mean, he never really wanted to part with any of his books. Or even let customers touch them. That's just not good business."

"True," said Cassandra. Although he was awesome at writing tragic plays, she'd always privately thought that running a bookstore had been a tragic *mistake* for him. He didn't really have the right people skills and was always hovering over customers, worried they might damage the scrollbooks for sale.

She grinned at her sister, nodding. "Yeah, but now who's going to tell the customers"—she deepened her voice to mimic Mr. Euripides' thick accent—"'You rip-uh deez books? You buy-uh deez books!'" Which of course made Laodice giggle.

Sure, he'd been a total worrywart, but Mr. Euripides had always been nice to her, thought Cassandra. And she didn't have many friends here in the Marketplace. Just one, really—a girl named Andromache who worked in a store called Magical Wagical that her aunt and uncle owned.

The store sold all kinds of magic things, including magic tattoos that constantly changed shape, cute magic dogs that never needed to be fed or walked, and Magic Answer Balls that tried to answer any question put to them. The store was way down at the other end of the IM.

Both Cassandra and Andromache had moved here from the city of Troy recently, after the Trojan War ended. Andromache had a special talent for baking and liked it way more than Cassandra did, so she hung out at the bakery as much as she could. Although she could be sweet and fun, she was kind of mad most of the time. And the target of her anger was always the same—the immortals on Mount Olympus. Which was actually something the two of them had in common. Because Cassandra was mad at the immortals too. Three of them, anyway!

As the construction workers began hanging cloths over the hole in the wall to cut down on dust in the bakery, Laodice elbowed her. "C'mon. It's almost time to open the store." Cassandra nodded and turned to follow her sister to the cookie counter.

"What's that?" her mom asked as Cassandra drew near.

Cassandra looked back over one shoulder to see a small piece of papyrus lying behind her on the floor. Argh! One of the fortunes had fallen from her pocket!

Her mom picked it up. When she realized what it was and read what was written on it, she frowned.

Laodice, who was a little ways beyond their mom now, shook her head at Cassandra. Her expression said, *Now you're in for it!*

"Cassie, dear! We've talked about this," Hecuba scolded. "No one wants to read your fortunes. Leave those to your brother to write."

Hecuba came closer and gave Cassandra a quick motherly hug, her voice softening. "Don't be jealous that he got the real talent for prophecy in this family. You need to accept that fortune-telling isn't something you're good at. Like I can't sing."

"And like I can't dance," Laodice put in matter-of-factly. Her sister really didn't have any sense of rhythm, Cassandra knew. But she was great with customers that came into the bakery. And Helenus was supposedly good at fortune-telling. So just exactly what was Cassandra good at? Getting into trouble, that's what!

Bam! Bam!

The sound of hammering drew Hecuba's attention to the giant hole in the wall again. "I want that doorway between the stores to be arched!" she shouted to the construction workers. "But don't put in an actual door. We want a free flow of traffic between the stores, so customers can take the cookies they buy with them while they browse the scrollbooks."

As she focused on the girls again, her eyes filled with excitement. "We'll call the new store Oracle-O Bakery and Scrollbooks! What do you think?"

"Sounds cool," said Laodice.

Cassandra wished she shared their enthusiasm. But though their mom was a super business whiz and loved running the bakery, the work left her with little time for family. And now with the store's expansion she'd have even *less* time to spare. Sometimes Cassandra couldn't help feeling like she took second place to the bakery in her mom's affections, or maybe even fourth place, after Laodice and her brother, too.

Without waiting for Cassandra to reply, Hecuba went on. "Hmm. We'll need to do a promotion—something special for our grand opening. Something attention-getting that's not too costly."

Her mom was always worrying about money problems. They'd paid a lot to buy the store from its previous owners, and now they were working hard to keep everything afloat. Her mom and dad had split up after the war, which is how Cassandra, Laodice, and Helenus had wound up here in the IM. Cassandra wanted the family bakery to succeed. Still, if business cratered, she couldn't help hoping it would mean they'd all get to move back to

Troy—and have things go back to how they used to be!

Suddenly Cassandra's nose wiggled a little. She sniffed the air and smelled—peppermints! Her eyes blinked, wider. As she stared into space, a new vision came to her. This time she saw a cocky teenage boy with blue hair that stuck straight up. He was sitting in Mr. Euripides' store—er, *their* store now—autographing scrollbooks tied with blue ribbons. Dozens and dozens of people were lining up to buy them.

There was a name on the poster next to him. Homer. She hadn't heard of him before, but he must be a big-time author. And judging by all the customers buying his books, this seemed like an awesome moneymaking scheme to her.

"I just got an idea for our grand opening," she began. "How about bringing a big megastar author into the store and—"

But before she could continue with her prophecy-inspired idea, her brother walked in through the front door of the bakery. "I'm having a vision," he announced.

Everyone, including the construction workers, froze in their tracks, breathlessly waiting to hear what he would say next. Cassandra rolled her eyes. It was so annoying that everyone cared what Helenus had to say when it came to fortune-telling but paid her prophecies no heed at all!

Basking in the attention, Helenus pressed two fingers to his forehead, concentrating hard. "I see a great event of monumental proportions with food, drink, and scrollbooks on hand," he said. "And a famous author to personally autograph the scrollbooks for the many customers that come into our store to buy."

Honestly! thought Cassandra. Once again he'd had the same idea as her! They often thought alike when it came to prophecies. She sometimes wondered if it was possible that his visions somehow fed off hers. Because he always seemed to have the same idea she'd had just seconds before. They were twins, but she'd been born first. Maybe that had something to do with it.

"Wonderful idea, Helenus!" their mom declared. It was like she hadn't even heard Cassandra saying the same thing only moments before! Her mom went over to Helenus, and the two continued off into the scrollbook store, discussing "his" idea.

Grrr. It really frustrated Cassandra that her brother's fortunes were always held in high regard by everyone and thought to be absolutely true without question. Hers, on the other hand, were dismissed as silliness, or worse— as lies!

Her twin was so lucky. He even got his own room because their older brother Hector was still back in Troy with their dad.

As Hecuba departed in a whirl of energy into the scrollbook shop, she called over her shoulder. "Please take care of the bakery today, girls. I'll have my hands full supervising the construction and making grand-opening plans. And, Cassandra, you'll need to bake some Oracle-Os for your brother's new fortunes."

Her mom nodded to the box that Helenus kept filled with the written prophecies he came up with. Those prophecies, scribbled down on slips of papyrus, would be placed inside cookies and distributed to mortal customers down on Earth.

However, the cookies that went up to the immortals (and a few lucky mortals) on Mount Olympus were magical and *spoke* their fortunes aloud instead. For those, Helenus would have to whisper a prophecy to each freshly baked cookie before it left the store. That task wouldn't take him long, however. Certainly not as long as it would take Cassandra to make the dough and bake the actual cookies!

"You have to admit, Helenus's idea for the grand opening is a good one," Laodice told Cassandra as the two girls finally got to work after their mom and brother left. Laodice began wiping construction dust off the top of the cookie counter and then started sharpening the quill pen they used to write receipts for purchases.

"Have you ever noticed how vague his prophecies are, though?" Cassandra asked as she dusted off the abacus they used to calculate change for paying customers. "Like, 'You will marry a man with a nice laugh.' Or, 'There will be a face on the moon the night before you meet the girl you will wed.' Sometimes they aren't even fortunes but only descriptions, like, 'You are kind to others.' Or, 'Others like you.' So the person who gets a fortune is flattered, and they're happy because they want to believe it's true."

"What's your point?" said Laodice.

"My point?" echoed Cassandra. "Isn't it obvious?"

"No," said Laodice.

Her point was that *her* fortunes were better! And she wasn't bragging. Not really. For example, she'd known the name of the author who would be at their grand opening—Homer. Her brother hadn't. Of course, she hadn't gotten the chance to tell anyone.

Feeling unappreciated, Cassandra went to the underground ice-room to get more of the cookie dough she'd made last night. A few minutes later, just as she began rolling the dough out in the small kitchen behind the counter to make the first of many batches of fortune cookies they'd bake and sell in the coming hours, the bell on the store's front door tinkled.

In walked their first customer of the day. A handsome teenage godboy. Laodice smiled at him and went to see if he needed help.

Cassandra made a fist and began pounding the cold cookie dough to soften it up. *Whomp!* She wished she could make her sister understand her frustrations. But although Laodice was only two years older than she was, she seemed to think of Cassandra as a little girl. A little girl without a care in the world and certainly no problems. Ha!

She did have problems—plenty of them. And in her opinion they'd all been caused by three immortals from Mount Olympus Academy—Athena, Aphrodite, and Apollo!

Whomp! As she pounded the dough, Cassandra thought about the trouble they'd made for her countrymen, meddling in their lives during the Trojan War. Not to mention all the trouble they'd caused her personally. But they probably thought nothing of it—if they ever even thought of her and Troy at all.

Cassandra automatically grabbed a rolling pin, dusted it with flour, and began rolling out the dough into a big flat pancake. Her friend Andromache said that the goddessgirls and godboys at Mount Olympus Academy didn't *have* any troubles. For them every day was nothing but fun, with parties and dancing and hardly any school-work.

Andromache also said that the Three A's (which was their secret code nickname for Athena, Aphrodite, and Apollo, since their names all started with the letter *A*) deserved a little payback for the trouble they'd caused Cassandra and other Trojans. She said that they deserved to have some troubles of their own!

After Cassandra put the cookies into the oven, she

patted her pocket, which was still full of the fortunes she'd written that morning. Andromache was right, she decided. And with the help of these prophecies, she was about to put her and Andromache's payback plan into effect!

2
The Payback Plan

Cassandra

THE BAKERY KEPT CASSANDRA BUSY ALL MORN-ing. So busy that she began to fear she wouldn't be able to sneak out to get her and Andromache's payback plan under way before it was time for school. She briefly considered skipping her first class. But the IM school was only in session three afternoons a week. Skipping would land her in big trouble. Besides, they were reading a scrollbook called *Dialogues* by an awesome philosopher named Plato in literature class, and she didn't want to miss the discussion.

When several batches of cookies were ready for fortunes, she dutifully took them to her brother Helenus, who had come to sit in the little office behind the bakery kitchen to do his job.

Meanwhile, one customer after another came and went from the store, drawn by the delicious smell of cookies and by curiosity about the fortunes they contained. Cassandra liked hearing the interesting news and gossip that shoppers from Earth, Mount Olympus, and other magical lands brought with them.

While she baked, she was listening with half an ear to their prattle, when she suddenly overheard someone say Athena's name. Her ears perked up. She looked over from her cookie trays to see that several boys about her age had come into the store. She knew them from school. Two of the boys were okay, but for some reason that Agamemnon was always teasing her.

"I think Athena must be his mentor," one of the boys with him was saying. "Odysseus is her Greek hero. So if he's heading back to his home in Ithaca now that the Trojan War is finally over, she must be helping him, right?"

Hmm, interesting, thought Cassandra. As she cleaned the prep table she'd been working on, she filed away that bit of information in a corner of her brain, thinking it might somehow help Andromache and her with their payback plan later on.

Then she hurried out to the cookie counter, since Laodice was busy helping Cleo, the purple-haired, three-eyed makeup lady who owned Cleo's Cosmetics in the IM. It sounded like Cleo was trying to find the perfect gift of cookies for Mr. Cyclops, a teacher at Mount Olympus Academy that she'd been dating.

Reluctantly Cassandra greeted the boys. "Welcome to the Oracle-O Bakery. Are you looking for anything special?"

"Uh-huh," Agamemnon told her. "Got any cookies in the shape of a horse?" He smirked at his friends and leaned an elbow on the counter next to where he was standing, acting all cooler than cool.

Ha. Ha. Ha, thought Cassandra. Like she hadn't heard that one before? She knew why he was teasing her like this. It was because she'd once predicted that an enormous wooden horse full of Greek soldiers, including Odysseus, would enter Troy and destroy it. No one had believed her about that Trojan horse. Not even after her prophecy had come true. Because after a little time had passed, her prophecy had gotten twisted around in everyone's minds. They thought she'd predicted just the opposite of what had actually happened!

"No, but I could make one shaped like a horse's behind, if you'll just let me draw your face as a cookie pattern," she replied. She smiled so brightly at Agamemnon that it took him a minute to realize she'd insulted him.

Straightening, he scowled. "Hey! What's that supposed to mean?"

"Sorry, no horses," said Laodice lightly, coming over now that Cleo had gone. She flashed a frown at Cassandra and shook her head, warning her to behave. Customers wouldn't come to the shop if word got around that the staff was mean!

"Yeah, sorry. My sister's right," Cassandra added, speaking to Agamemnon in the same supersweet voice she'd used before. "So maybe you and your friends should just gallop on out of here before I bring you bad luck. Because, though I don't mean to, I do it sometimes."

When she saw good fortune in someone's future, it was her pleasure to tell them. But when she saw bad fortune, she felt obligated to warn them too. Either way, people might halfway believe her fortunes in the beginning, but as time passed, they changed their minds and decided she'd gotten things wrong! Not only that, but they often decided she was kind of to blame if anything bad happened, so she'd gotten a reputation for being bad luck. She just couldn't win!

At her words, the boys' expressions had turned uncomfortable and a little scared. Mumbling something about needing to go buy a new shield at Mighty Fighty—an IM store that sold battle and athletic stuff— Agamemnon's two friends shuffled out the door and hurried off. Unfortunately, Agamemnon stuck around.

As Cassandra got back to work, she felt him glancing

over at her now and then as he wandered around the store, checking out the different kinds of cookies for sale. She couldn't understand why he was still there. Didn't he believe she was bad luck? His friends obviously did. She'd known that and had played on their fears to make them leave.

Some people went out of their way to avoid her, as if she were a black cat. Or a ladder they needed to walk around. Though she used their nervousness to her advantage sometimes, it also kind of hurt her feelings.

Cassandra's *own* luck hadn't been the best lately, but she believed you could make your own luck. And that's what she was about to do, just as soon as she could take action. As in, get out of here to run a very important errand. A payback one!

"All done," Helenus announced. He'd just come in from the back office and set a box of spoken-fortune cookies on the counter next to a box with his written fortunes.

Noticing Agamemnon, his face brightened. "Hey, what's up?" he asked. "Want to go to Mighty Fighty? I heard they got in some new swords."

Grrr. Her brother didn't seem to care that Agamemnon had been on their enemies' side during the Trojan War.

"Sure," said Agamemnon, shrugging agreeably.

Laodice started trying to cheer her up the minute Helenus and Agamemnon left the store. "Don't let those boys get to you. You know why Agamemnon teases you, right?"

"Because he's a dork?" Cassandra guessed.

Ding! At the sound of the timer bell, she zipped over to the oven and pulled out the current batch of freshly baked cookies. She set them on the cooling rack.

"No. Because he likes you," said Laodice.

Huh? Then he was wasting his time hanging around. No way she would ever like that boy back, Cassandra thought, totally underwhelmed by this information. Agamemnon was a bully.

"So he's mean to me because he likes me?" asked Cassandra. "That's ridiculous. No, wait, it's worse than that. It's ri*donk*ulous."

Laodice smiled at her in a superior sort of way. "That's how some boys are. Show-offs at times. Anyway, I think he's kind of cute. Thirteen's too young for me, of course."

Cassandra rolled her eyes. Laodice's mind was always on boys these days. Right now she was mostly crushing on an older teenage boy who worked in Mr. Dolos's Be A Hero store. It sold all kinds of products like drinking mugs and posters with autographed pictures of mortal heroes on them. Last week she'd been crushing on Cleo's son, and the week before that it had been someone else.

Well, that was fine for her, but Cassandra had had enough trouble from boys in her life so far! Especially from one particular immortal—that Apollo, who was the godboy of prophecy, among other things. When they'd both been little kids—her in kindergarten and him in first grade—they'd happened to meet in a temple. And Apollo had put a curse on her! He'd proclaimed that her prophecies would forever after be thought true at first and then quickly be judged to be false. No one had believed any of her predictions ever since.

It was *sooo* not fair! she thought. But Andromache claimed that all immortals were stuck-up and didn't care about mortals like them.

Like Apollo, Aphrodite sure didn't seem to care. She was the one who had made Cassandra's other brother, Paris, fall in love with a Greek queen named Helen. It was their romance that had started the Trojan War in the first place.

But maybe what Athena had done was worst of all. She'd sent the Trojan horse. When it had entered the gates of Troy, the Greek heroes inside it had leaped out and attacked the city. Led by Athena's special hero, Odysseus himself!

Cassandra had tried to warn everyone what would happen if the Trojan horse were allowed into the city. But because of the curse Apollo had brought down on her head in that temple seven years before, no one had been willing to believe her.

This was the horse prophecy Agamemnon had been talking about. The one everyone remembered. Cassandra's biggest, most embarrassing flop! Her face heated just thinking about it.

Hearing another *ding*, she pulled a new batch of cookies from the oven. She peeked over her shoulder as she worked. Laodice was busy with a new customer. Her mom was over in the scrollbook store talking to the construction guys. Helenus was gone. The coast was clear.

Still, she hesitated to put the payback plan into motion. It really wasn't her nature to be mean to anyone, but she was just so frustrated about everything! And Andromache agreed that the Three A's were to blame for her seven years of bad luck. She couldn't back out on the payback plan now, right? She couldn't let Andromache down.

Quickly Cassandra pulled the papyrus fortunes she'd written that morning from her pocket and set them on the counter. After folding one fortune in half, she set it atop a warm, round cookie. Then she set a second cookie on top and gently pressed, sealing the two cookies together around the edges with the prophecy inside. It was like a cookie sandwich with a papyrus fortune filling.

She did the same with the others, until each of her fortunes was hidden inside a cookie. She wished she could've spoken her fortunes as Helenus had done, but then Laodice or her mom would've heard her do it and known she was up to something. So the papyrus fortunes would have to do. After wrapping each finished cookie, she set them on top of Helenus's spoken-fortune cookies in the basket bound for MOA.

She wasn't worried about the students there getting the right fortunes. Her fortunes were stronger than those of her brother, no matter what everyone else thought. If anyone at MOA took a cookie, they would get the right fortune. And if she *hadn't* written a fortune for someone and Helenus had, they'd get *his* fortune.

"Cassandra?" called her mom.

Cassandra's head jerked up, her eyes wide. Had she been caught in the act? "Yeah, Mom?"

Phew! Turned out that her mom only had an errand for her to run. "Take a dozen cookies down to Ms. Demeter's store in trade for some flour, will you?" she told Cassandra. Demeter was Persephone's mom and owned an IM store that sold all kinds of plants as well as basic cooking ingredients made from plants—like wheat flour! "And while you're at it, drop off that MOA cookie delivery to Hermes' Delivery Service on your way," Hecuba added.

"Okay!" Cassandra called back. *Yay! Perfect timing!*

She snatched up the basket of fortune cookies and a smaller box of cookies to trade with Ms. Demeter. Then she zipped out the front door of the store and into the Immortal Marketplace.

Not only was the IM enormous, but it was amazingly beautiful, with a sparkling high-ceilinged crystal roof. Rows and rows of columns separated the various shops selling everything from the newest Greek fashions to tridents and thunderbolts.

She dashed through the atrium, past a merrily splashing fountain encircled with blooming rhododendron bushes. She waved to Cleo through the front window of Cleo's Cosmetics but didn't stop to admire the new outfits in the window of the Green Scene, a store where all the clothes for sale were green. And she didn't linger to gaze at the magical gifts in the window of Gods' Gift like she usually did, or to look at the merchandise displayed in any of the other stores along the Marketplace. Because today she was on a mission!

She glimpsed a sundial through one of the side glass door exits. It was three minutes till noon as she flew right past Demeter's Daisies, Daffodils, and Floral Delights, where she was supposed to barter fresh cookies for flour to make even more cookies. Her family traded with other shopkeepers in the Marketplace for things they needed. But she'd have to take care of that errand later. First she had to catch Hermes before noon when he left with his daily deliveries to Mount Olympus Academy and other destinations.

She put on a burst of speed, passing Hera's Happy Endings, a wedding store. Inside, Cassandra could see the beautiful and statuesque goddess Hera giving advice to a lady trying on white veils. She must be planning a wedding.

Hera, of course, was married to Zeus—the principal of MOA, King of the Gods and Ruler of the Heavens. Thinking about Zeus reminded Cassandra of Athena, Zeus's daughter. The person who'd made her a laughing-stock. She hurried on, determined to outpace her unhappy thoughts.

Everyone else in Cassandra's family seemed to have gotten past the events of the Trojan War and the part the immortals had played in them, but she simply couldn't let those things go. She missed her home in Troy so much. There she'd been a princess living in a palace, instead of in a few crowded rooms above a store. Plus, she'd had some friends, even if they had mostly been chosen by her parents.

As Cassandra passed Magical Wagical, Andromache ducked her head out of the store to give her a thumbs-up. "You go, girl!" she called encouragingly.

"Thanks!" said Cassandra, her spirits improving. Although Andromache didn't think Cassandra's fortunes were accurate, she did believe they could stir up trouble. And that girl really had it in for the immortals. Way more than Cassandra did. She was behind their payback plan all the way.

Of course, their plan wasn't meant to hurt anyone or make *big* trouble. They just wanted to cause a little dismay among MOA students, especially the Three A's. Neither she nor Andromache were sure what would happen as a result of the fortunes she was sending to MOA, which was kind of worrisome. And there was one fortune that had Cassandra more than a little unsettled. One of the two she was sending to Zeus himself! It read simply: *Carousel.* What was that about? She really didn't know!

She was almost at the Hermes' Delivery Service headquarters at the far end of the Marketplace. She craned her neck, trying to see ahead. Hermes' silver-winged delivery chariot was already piled high with packages beyond the two glass doors that led outside the IM. She watched as he bustled from his office out to the chariot, adding one last load before he would take off for Earth, Mount Olympus Academy, and other magical lands.

Oh, no! She had to catch him before he left. The

cookies with her fortunes would be stale by tomorrow and get thrown away. She put on a burst of speed. "Wait!" she called. But he couldn't hear her from outside.

A dozen steps later she burst out of the IM's glass doors. The chariot's wings had begun to flap. Hermes was starting to lift off.

"Incoming!" she shouted to him. Bounding for the chariot, she lobbed the basket of cookies high. *Plunk!* They sailed into the chariot. "It's the Oracle-O cookie order for MOA!"

Hermes just grunted down at her, impatient as usual. Ignoring the dark look he sent her, she grinned back and waved. "Thanks!" she called as he lifted off.

Smiling to herself, Cassandra watched his chariot until it was only a speck in the sky, disappearing into the clouds. Would those immortals take the bait hidden inside the cookies she'd crafted especially for them?

3

Cookie Fortunes

Athena

ATHENA JUGGLED THE TWO SCROLLS SHE WAS
carrying in one arm and peeked ahead in the MOA
cafeteria lunch line as she pushed her tray along with her
free hand. It was Thursday afternoon, and after a long
morning of classes she was mega-hungry!

Spotting a familiar basket with the Oracle-O Bakery
logo on it at the end of the line, she took a deep breath,

inhaling the delicious chocolaty bakery smell. "Mmm," she said, closing her blue-gray eyes briefly in delight. Speaking to Aphrodite, who was just ahead of her, she said, "That basket of cookies smells yummy."

Aphrodite's golden hair swung forward, and she flipped it over her shoulder as she glanced back at Athena. "I'm drooling over them too. I hope there are some left by the time we get up there!"

"If not, I'm sure any boy in the cafeteria would rush to give you his," Athena commented. She wasn't just saying that. Boys were always falling over themselves to snag Aphrodite's attention. She was the goddessgirl of love and beauty—the most beautiful goddessgirl at Mount Olympus Academy! Even now, a godboy who was a centaur, with hooves instead of feet, was gazing at her in admiration. Yet she hardly even noticed.

The two goddessgirl friends moved along with their

trays, both getting the ambrosia salad and a carton of nectar to drink. At the end of the line Aphrodite reached into the Oracle-O basket, then drew her hand back in surprise. She gave a little laugh as she reached in again and took the cookie that rolled into her grasp.

Athena reached into the basket too. The magical cookies shifted around, one of them edging closer to her hand than all the others. She took the cookie that seemed to want to be hers.

Once the girls got to their usual table, they sat in the two empty chairs across from Persephone. Athena noticed she'd gotten a cookie too. They were irresistible! Plus it was fun to hear the fortunes.

"Remember when Oracle-Os used to freak you out?" Persephone said, spotting the cookie on Athena's tray.

"Not anymore," said Athena, poking a straw into her carton of nectar. "When I first came to MOA, they kind of did because, well, who wants to eat food that talks? But once I realized they weren't really alive or anything, I fell in love with them!"

Persephone grinned and nodded, which made her long, curly red ponytail bounce. "Me too."

"Me three," added Aphrodite, and they all laughed.

Seeing Artemis enter the cafeteria, Athena sent her a little wave. As usual Artemis's glossy black hair was caught up in a cute, simple twist high at the back of her head that was encircled by golden bands.

And also as usual, her favorite archery bow hung over one shoulder and a tooled leather quiver of arrows was slung across her back. Not that she needed those in order to eat lunch, but she was rarely without them. Of course, Athena didn't really need to bring scrolls to lunch either, but she liked having something to read nearby at all times.

Athena took a long, cool drink of nectar. Instantly her skin began to shimmer a little more brightly. When immortals drank nectar, it caused that effect. It never made her roommate Pandora's skin sparkle, though, or Medusa's. Because although those girls went to MOA too, they were mortals.

Just then Artemis sat down opposite Athena at their table.

"Looks like we all have a sweet tooth today," Persephone said, nodding toward the cookie on Artemis's tray.

"Yeah, what can I say? It was calling my name." Artemis grinned. She held the wrapped cookie up in one hand near her mouth. Pitching her voice higher than normal, she pretended she was the cookie, saying, "Artemis! Artemis! Eat meee!"

Which, of course, made the others giggle so hard that Athena almost spurted nectar out of her nose! Heads turned their way at the sound, faces smiling at them. The four girls were among the most popular students at MOA and were all best friends. Each of them had their own special style and different interests, but all wore a gold necklace with a dangling double-G-shaped charm.

After finishing her meal, Athena unwrapped her Oracle-O cookie. She waited for it to speak a fortune. It didn't. "Hey," she said in disappointment. "I think my cookie's a dud."

"So's mine," said Aphrodite. There was a puzzled look on her face as she stared at it.

Athena took a bite of her cookie anyway. "Whah?" Tasting something weird, she quickly pulled the cookie away from her mouth. A little piece of papyrus was sticking out of it!

"Look!" she said, showing the others.

"There's one in mine, too," said Persephone.

50

"Mine, too," Aphrodite said at the same time. "The fortunes must be written on them."

After pulling the slip of papyrus from her cookie, Athena read it aloud: "'A horse, of course.'"

"What kind of a fortune is that?" Persephone said, laughing.

"I have no clue," said Athena. She flipped it over. "There's part of a drawing on the back, but I can't tell what it's of."

"Let's see what mine says," said Aphrodite. She pulled out the slip and read it aloud. "'You have no fashion sense.'" Her brow furrowed, and she looked up at the others. "Huh? That's not a fortune. Besides, it's just plain wrong."

Athena had to agree. Aphrodite was absolutely obsessed with clothes and had a different outfit for almost every activity, sometimes changing her clothes five times a day. Right now she was completely color-coordinated and looked dazzling in the hot-pink chiton she was wearing. Her gleaming golden hair, threaded with sparkly pink ribbons, hung down her back in loose curls. Even her nail polish matched. Each fingernail was hot pink with a little heart decoration that flashed with glitter. She was such a trendsetter that probably every other goddessgirl at school would be wearing polish just like that before the week was out!

Now Persephone held up her fortune. "Mine says 'Your green thumb will turn brown,'" she announced. She frowned at the slip of papyrus. "That can't be right."

Persephone was the goddessgirl of growing things. Green things with lots of flowers, not brown, dead-looking things. In fact, a new hybrid flower she'd recently created to grow in the hot, harsh conditions of the Underworld had been accepted into the famous Anthestiria Flower Festival!

Just then Principal Zeus entered the cafeteria. A teenage mortal boy with spiky blue hair trailed him. The boy was talking a mile a minute and seemed to be trying to convince Zeus of something. Mortals were always asking Athena's dad for stuff. After all, he was a powerful guy—the King of the Gods and Ruler of the Heavens, not to mention the principal of MOA!

What could this boy want? He probably had some big idea he wanted Zeus to finance. Maybe some temple he wanted Zeus to build? Whatever it was, the boy likely wouldn't succeed in getting her dad's backing. Zeus liked to come up with his own ideas.

"I wonder who that blue-haired boy with my dad is?" she said aloud. "The one with a determined scholarly look about him, carrying a scrollbook tied with a blue ribbon in one hand."

"His name is Homer," a voice informed her. Athena

glanced around to see that Pheme, the goddessgirl of gossip, had come over to their table. The tips of her cute new glittery wings, which Zeus had recently given her, fluttered gently at her back. They were orange, just like her short hair, lip gloss, and the chiton she wore today.

Athena scrunched her face, trying to remember where she'd heard the name Homer recently.

"He's an up-and-coming author," Pheme supplied. The words she spoke puffed from her lips as cloud-letters and rose to hover above her head, where anyone looking could read them. "He wrote that scrollbook he's carrying. It's not actually published yet. It's called *The Iliad* and will be for sale beginning next weekend."

Athena snapped her fingers. "Oh, that's right. I read a review of *The Iliad* just yesterday in the *Greekly Weekly News*." She frowned as she recalled a particular detail that had been left out of the review.

"What's it about?" asked Aphrodite.

"The Trojan War," said Pheme. Then she looked at Athena a little uncertainly, as if unsure of her facts. "Right?"

Athena nodded. Everyone considered her the brainiest student at MOA, so she was used to others asking her for information. "It's actually an elongated poem written in dactylic hexameter," she told Pheme. "Which is a rhythmic form of poetic meter authors sometimes use."

"Really?" Pheme's eyes grew excited. Immediately she dashed off to spread this new info about Zeus's guest.

Athena had to hide a smile when she overheard Pheme speaking to another group of girls one table over. The words floating above the gossipy girl's head read: *It's a long gated poem about pterodactyl hexes!*

Artemis glanced toward the young author as she unwrapped *her* cookie. "What do you think he's doing here at MOA?" she asked the other three girls.

"Probably something to do with *The Iliad*, that scroll-book he wrote. Even though it's not in stores yet, it has been getting lots of press," Athena explained to her friends. "According to the review I read, his work's not altogether accurate, though."

As Artemis munched her cookie, she asked, "What do you mean?"

Athena huffed a frustrated sigh, which ruffled a few strands of her long brown hair. "It's just that his scroll-book is about the Trojan War, right? Well, guess what he left out?" Before her friends could guess, Athena told them. "My Trojan horse."

"Huh?" asked Persephone, her brows going up. "How can you write a book about the Trojan War without including the very thing that put an end to it?"

"Exactly!" said Athena.

"Hey, look, I got a papyrus fortune too," Artemis

announced, drawing out the slip from her half-eaten cookie. She read it aloud. "'Your arrow will miss its target five times in a row.'"

"Ha! That's nuts!" said Apollo, who'd happened by and overheard. "You've never missed a target five times in a row in your life!" he added. He was Artemis's twin brother, and the two of them practiced archery almost every day.

"You got that right," Artemis agreed. She stuck up one hand and gave her brother a quick high five.

"These fortunes are all weird. Here's mine," Apollo said, pulling a papyrus slip from the pocket of his tunic. "'Your curse you should reverse.'"

Athena noticed that his and Artemis's fortunes had partial drawings on the backs of them too. Cocking her head at him, she asked, "What curse?"

"That's the thing," said Apollo. "As far as I know, I've

never cursed anything or anyone in my life. I mean, I cast a spell or two in Spell-ology class when I took it in first grade, but what immortal hasn't?"

As Apollo went off with his friends, Athena glanced over at her dad in time to see him spot the Oracle-Os. His blue eyes widened with delight, and he made a bee-line for the basket. After taking a couple of cookies, Zeus turned and headed toward the goddessgirls' table on his way to an exit door. Had he only come to the cafeteria for snacks? He did have a major sweet tooth.

A jolt of excitement filled Athena as Homer followed in Zeus's wake, still talking away. Homer might not be the most accurate author on Earth, but he was poised to become a megastar in the publishing world. She could hardly wait to read his scrollbook, in spite of the fact that it bugged her that he had chosen to leave out her Trojan horse. That horse had been her idea, and like Persephone had said, it seemed to her that it had won the war. What kind of author left out important facts like that? She wanted to ask him but suddenly felt a little shy as he and her dad halted in front of her and her friends' table.

"So, as I was saying," Homer was boasting to Zeus, "The *Iliad* reviews have been amazing. Stunning, really, if I do say so myself. Some reviewers have called it an epic scrollbook. Destined to become a classic." He whipped out copies of *Teen Scrollazine* and *Greekly Weekly News* from a satchel he carried, and pointed out the reviews. "Perhaps you'd like to read them for yourself?"

But Zeus wasn't listening. His attention was focused on the first of the Oracle-O cookies as he unwrapped it.

"*The Iliad* releases next weekend, and I'd love to make a big splash," Homer went on, not at all discouraged by Zeus's refusal to read the reviews. "What better location to begin my author tour than right here at Mount

Olympus Academy? We can have a big event with balloons and food. What do you say?"

By now Zeus had discovered the papyrus fortune inside his cookie. "What's this?" His bushy red eyebrows knit together as he read aloud: "'Make a splash with your next bash. Hold it at the scrollbook shop in the Immortal Marketplace!'"

Suddenly Zeus's face lit with excitement. He put much faith in oracles, fortunes, and prophecies. Now he turned to Homer and clapped a big hand on the young author's shoulder, causing an electrical spark that made the author wince. "I just had an amazing idea, Homie," he said. "We'll do your book signing at the Immortal Marketplace. We'll make it a big splashy bash with food and fun. Sound good?"

Homie? Did her dad not know the author's actual name? Athena wondered. Maybe not. He was really bad with names. From Homie's—er, Homer's—expression, Athena could see that he was a little disappointed by Zeus's suggestion. He wanted the event to be held here at Mount Olympus Academy. It was a more prestigious location for sure.

"That's an awesome idea of course," Homer said, being careful not to insult Zeus. "However, wouldn't it make more sense to hold my book release extravaganza here at MOA? At the very place where students in Hero-ology classes helped direct the events of the Trojan War that are described in *The Iliad*? Your students would benefit too. They can study my scrollbook in their classes. And ask me questions about writing and being an author. It's a great opportunity for them and me. What do you say?"

Zeus's blazing blue eyes narrowed at the author. Tiny sparks of electricity began to prickle all along his muscled arms. Sure signs that her dad was annoyed. It was always best to agree with his ideas, unless you could make him think that your ideas were *his*.

Homer was no fool. Immediately a big fake-looking smile spread across his face. "On second thought, I love your suggestion!" he said. "After all, the Immortal Marketplace is halfway between the Earth and the heavens—the next best thing to Mount Olympus itself. I'm sure you have even more ideas that would make the event superspecial. So do I. So maybe we . . ."

While half-listening to the blue-haired author prattle on, Zeus tried his second cookie. He read the fortune silently. "Carousel?" he boomed in his loud voice. He looked up from the fortune, his expression a little puzzled. He surveyed the faces of the students around him, and then his eyes came to rest on Athena.

"Oh, I get it," she said, thinking fast. "'Carou*sell*' with the emphasis on the 'sell.' Is that what you're thinking,

Dad? Building a carousel at the amazing event you came up with to help sell Homer's new scrollbook?"

Zeus's eyes lit up. "Right! What a great idea I had! And here's another one." After scanning the cafeteria, he began to point to students at random, calling out names. In all he chose about twenty students, including Athena and her three BFFs.

"Each of you," he said at last to the ones he'd selected, "are excused from classes all next week. I'm going to place a magical carousel in the Immortal Marketplace. And *you* will decorate it." At this, excited murmurs ran though the gathered students.

"You'll each choose a favorite animal and build a carousel-size statue of it that kids can ride," he went on. "You will imbue it with magic to thrill mortals who come to the Immortal Marketplace for the book event."

"What if someone doesn't want to do an animal?"

Pandora called out, even though she wasn't among the chosen students. She was always asking Zeus questions when no one else dared to, so he was pretty used to it and didn't get mad.

"If you don't want to do an animal, just help decorate the carousel itself. It must be finished by—" He lifted an eyebrow in Homer's direction.

"My scrollbook will be in stores next Saturday," Homer informed him.

"By next Saturday, then." Suddenly filled with creative energy, Zeus zoomed toward the cafeteria exit. "Hera is going to love this idea. All the extra visitors to the IM should help boost sales at her wedding store. Can't wait to tell her! Let's go down to the IM and get that carousel started. C'mon, Homie."

Looking delighted at Zeus's enthusiasm, Homer followed him out the cafeteria door. Once they'd gone, the twenty chosen students began buzzing with ideas for carousel animals.

"Dibs on dog," Hades said quickly. He looked at Ares, whose mouth was hanging open as if he were about to argue. "Sorry, god-dude," Hades told him, "but Cerberus is the biggest, baddest dog around. Mortals will love being able to ride a carousel animal that looks like him!"

Hades was god of the Underworld, and Cerberus was the three-headed dog that guarded the place. Huge and snarling, the dog was pretty scary until you got to know him. Athena figured Hades was right that kids would get a kick out of a Cerberus carousel ride.

Many of the immortal students had more than one favorite animal, and the dog was one of Ares' and Artemis's favorites too. Ares' eyes narrowed at Hades, but then he gave in and claimed a different animal. "Owl," he said.

Athena gaped at him, her eyes as big and round as an owl's. "Huh?" Everyone knew the owl was *her* favorite animal. Because it symbolized wisdom. She had all kinds of owl stuff, like the cute owl earrings she was wearing now. She could even shape-shift into a real owl!

Of course, she couldn't really argue with Ares' choice. She didn't own the idea of owls or anything, and apparently Ares liked owls too.

All around her, other students were rushing to decide on animals, each naming the one they liked best. Dionysus decided on leopard, Hephaestus chose donkey, and Apollo went with raven.

"I'm going to do a swan ride," said Aphrodite. Which was perfect, since she actually had a magical swan cart that could fly. Artemis chose deer, since she had golden-horned deer that led her chariot. And Poseidon, who was godboy of the sea, went with dolphin. Another student named Pan, who was the godboy of shepherding, chose a sheep.

Iris was having trouble coming up with an animal, so she volunteered to help decorate the carousel with the colors of the rainbow, which was her goddess symbol.

"And I'll make carved swags of flowers and greenery along the top and bottom of the carousel," said Persephone. "Maybe I'll paint a black-and-white kitten here and there too." She and Aphrodite shared a kitten named Adonis, so Athena knew Persephone must have been thinking of him when she'd added that last.

Athena overheard Heracles saying he'd do a lion statue. *Figures,* she thought fondly. He'd saved many mortals from a rampaging lion once. And now he wore its skin like a cloak. Medusa, who had snakes for hair, chose to do—what else but a big serpent! She'd need help instilling magic into her statue, though. Since she was a mortal, she had no magical powers of her own.

Persephone, Aphrodite, and Artemis gathered around Athena, looking concerned.

"I think Ares should change his choice. He's not being fair to choose the one animal that everyone knows you like best," Artemis said to Athena.

"Want me to talk to him?" Aphrodite offered. "I know he likes vultures, too. Maybe I could get him to change his mind."

"No, it's okay," said Athena. Aphrodite was Ares' crush, so she might be able to persuade him. But Athena didn't want to be a bad sport.

"Then what are you going to do?" asked Persephone.

Suddenly an idea came to Athena, and she heard herself say, "A horse, of course."

"The Trojan horse? Why, that's perfect!" said Aphrodite. She clapped her hands together in delight. "It goes so nicely with the theme of Homer's new book."

Athena hadn't exactly meant that. But what Aphrodite said made sense, so she nodded, feeling herself becoming more enthusiastic. She'd use Woody, a toy wooden horse she'd brought from home when she'd first come to MOA, as a model for the horse on the carousel.

"Hey, wait a minute," she said suddenly. She pulled the cookie fortune from her tray and smoothed it out. "'A horse, of course,'" she read aloud.

She looked at the others in surprise. "I think my fortune just came true!"

4

Hero-ology

Athena

ATHENA HAD ONLY JUST SAT DOWN IN HER FIRST period Hero-ology class the next morning when Medusa, who sat across the aisle, sent her a mischievous grin. "Better check the game board. Your Greek hero headed north from Troy and raided the island of the Cicones for supplies last night."

"Oh, no! After ten years of war he must be so anxious

to get home that he's taking foolish chances," said Athena. She made a beeline for the giant game board that stood in the center of the room, so she could check on her mortal hero.

She immediately spotted Odysseus's twelve ships in the Aegean Sea on the far side of the board, which covered the top of a table about the size of two Ping-Pong tables set side by side. The game board's three-dimensional world map showed colorful countries dotted with turreted castles, cozy villages, winding roads, and green hills. The countries were surrounded by oceans filled with little sea monsters, mermaids, and scaly dragons that really moved!

Dozens of three-inch-tall hero statues stood atop the board here and there as moveable game pieces. Each hero was always working toward a goal, but also trying to outdo the others. Immortal students were supposed to guide their mortal figures and were graded on how well they did it.

But like other students, Athena had four other classes at MOA plus homework. And Cheer as an extra-curricular too. So she couldn't watch over her hero day and night. Which meant that sometimes he got himself into trouble when she wasn't looking. It was her job to get him back out of it!

Now that the Trojan War was over—the brave Odysseus had won it earlier in the year with the help of her Trojan horse trick—he and his soldiers were travel-ing home to the city of Ithaca in Greece. The trouble he was in now was her fault, she decided. She should've provided the things he and his men required for their voyage, like food, drink, rope, tools, and sailcloth, yes-terday before they'd left. Then he and his men wouldn't have *needed* to raid the Cicones for supplies.

Thunk! As Athena studied Odysseus's position on the board, something struck the ground by her feet, spraying her with a mist of water. "What the—"

She looked over to see that Poseidon had slammed the handle end of his pitchforklike trident on the floor, its three sharp prongs pointed up. Water was dribbling down it to puddle at his feet. He pulled the pointy prong end back and then gave it a shove. It whipped toward the board, striking the edge of it. On the game board map the Aegean Sea suddenly turned choppy.

"Oops!" he said, not looking at all sorry. He'd obviously done that on purpose just to make trouble.

Odysseus's ships bounced around crazily, water sloshing over their decks. Poseidon, who pretty much ruled the seas, had stirred the waters with a mere whack of his trident.

"Stop it!" Athena told him. Since whatever happened

to a hero on the board actually happened to the real-life hero down on Earth, Poseidon's actions were creating an actual storm and swamping Odysseus's real ships!

Poseidon just grinned at her, unrepentant.

Athena bent toward the board and cupped her hands and forearms around the dozen ships. She scooted the whole fleet farther southwest into the Mediterranean Sea.

"Nice save," said Poseidon in a snarky voice.

Athena sighed. What was his problem? She really didn't want to fight him every class. "Look, I know it bugs you that I made an A plus on our last project. But just because I did, that doesn't mean you can't make one too. It's not like Mr. Cyclops only hands out one top grade per project. If we work together, maybe we'll both make A pluses!"

"Hmph!" muttered Poseidon. "Not gonna happen. Because my new assignment, now that the war is over, is to stop your hero from reaching Ithaca! So only one of us can win. And I'm going to beat you this time." With that, he slung his drippy trident over one shoulder and ambled off.

Aphrodite came to stand beside her. "I heard that," she said in a low voice. "And it's not just your high grades that are the problem, you know. Ever since your olive bested his water park in the Invention Fair and the people of Athens named their city for you instead of calling it Poseidonville, he hasn't been able to get over it."

"I know. He's sooo competitive," Athena replied. She leaned over the board to study her hero's new situation, then whisked his ships to an island in northern Africa inhabited by the lotus-eaters. Odysseus and his crew could rest there while checking their ships for damage.

"Poseidon's going to keep making trouble for us," Aphrodite warned.

Still surveying the game board, Athena nodded. "I know."

During the Trojan War, she and Aphrodite had been on opposite sides. Not anymore, though. Now that the war was over, the romance that Aphrodite's hero Paris had begun with the beautiful Helen was over too. So in her role as goddess of love, Aphrodite was now helping Odysseus's wife, Penelope, instead. Because that woman was in big trouble. When Odysseus got home to Ithaca, he would have a lot to fix.

That is, if he ever did get home. Poseidon seemed determined to stop Athena's hero from succeeding at that task. Keeping Odysseus away from home was his best chance to get the better of her.

"Where'd that outfit come from? The mismatch patch?" Medusa asked out of nowhere.

What was she talking about? Athena glanced over her

shoulder and saw that Medusa, Apollo, and a few other students had come over to check on the board.

And apparently it was Aphrodite who Medusa had been speaking to. *Whoa!* Athena had been so intent on the game board that she hadn't actually looked at Aphrodite yet this morning. Now that she did, her jaw dropped.

Because Aphrodite was wearing a chiton patterned with huge neon-orange, purple, and black flowers. And she'd paired it with red sandals, a green belt, and brown earrings. Her favorite color was pink, but there wasn't a speck of pink anywhere to be seen. Medusa was right. That mismatched outfit was so not her!

"What's wrong?" Aphrodite asked. She glanced from Medusa to Athena and back to Medusa again, her expression confused.

"Your fashion sense has turned to *non*sense," said

Medusa. "That's what's wrong." She folded her arms, looking suspicious. Was she worried that the outfit Aphrodite wore was meant to trick or tease her? Medusa often acted like she thought whatever weird things others did were somehow about *her*.

"Maybe she's just trying something different," Athena suggested gently, even though Aphrodite's outfit was so loud and bright, it almost hurt her eyes. "Nothing wrong with that."

"Huh? What are you two talking about?" Aphrodite looked down at her outfit. When she saw herself, a horrified little shriek escaped her. "Ye gods! What was I thinking?"

She turned toward Athena, her blue eyes wide. "It was that cookie fortune! *'You have no fashion sense.'* Remember? I was up so late thinking about it that I was only half awake when I chose this outfit—an outfit I would never,

ever in a million years normally wear on purpose."

"Sure looks like the prediction came true," Medusa said.

Athena's eyes sharpened thoughtfully. "And mine came true yesterday."

"Something's definitely up with those cookies," said Apollo, eyeing Aphrodite's loud outfit doubtfully. It seemed that even he could tell it had been a bad choice! "In archery practice after school yesterday, guess how many times Artemis missed the target?"

"Five?" asked Athena.

"Right you are," said Apollo. "Exactly five, just like her fortune foretold. But then she hit every bull's-eye after that."

"You know, I got one of those cookies yesterday too. I never opened it, but it's in my bag," Medusa admitted. She went over to her desk, and when she came back, she was holding a cookie. She ripped off its wrapper, broke open the cookie, and then silently read the fortune that had been inside. Rolling her eyes, she handed off her fortune to Athena and began breaking up the cookie into a bunch of small pieces.

Athena read the fortune aloud. "It says, 'Nobody will make you giggle.'"

Everyone looked at Medusa, watching as she tossed the cookie pieces into the air overhead. *Snap! Snap!* Her twelve snakes chomped every crumb before a single one could fall to the floor.

"That's dumb," she said to the group, dusting the last crumbs from her hands. "I *never* giggle."

Athena wasn't sure that was entirely true, but before she could get into a discussion about the fortune, someone bumped her shoulder. Poseidon had come up beside her. And the teacher was with him!

"See what I mean, Mr. Cyclops?" Poseidon said, directing the teacher's attention to the game board. "Athena's hero and his crew just landed on Cyclops Island and sneaked into your brother's cave. The must be after his food."

Athena whipped around just in time to see the last of Odysseus's men enter the cave on the board. *Ye gods!* Poseidon was right. While *her* attention had been on the Oracle-O fortunes, *Poseidon's* had obviously been on the game board. She couldn't turn her back on that Odysseus for a minute! He was in such a hurry to get back to his wife, Penelope, and son, Telemachus, in Ithaca that he was blundering around on his own instead of waiting for her help.

Mr. Cyclops's single eye blinked at Athena. "This is unacceptable," he told her in a disapproving voice.

"I know. It's my fault," Athena admitted. "I sailed

Odysseus and his men way too far in one push without giving them enough food. I'm sure they didn't mean any harm. They're just hungry!"

"And thirsty," Aphrodite added.

Poseidon folded his arms. "They still shouldn't steal."

He was right, of course. And if her hero was stealing from the teacher's *brother*, which he probably was, that was an extra bad idea! If she wanted a good grade, that is.

Before she could apologize on behalf of her hero, a glittery, magical wind whooshed in through the classroom window. *Message for Mr. Cyclops!* it called out in a huffy-puffy voice.

"Here!" said Mr. Cyclops, crooking a finger at it. The wind whooshed around the room, messing up hairdos and blowing textscrolls off desks just for fun, before stopping in front of the teacher to recite its message:

I trapped a crew that came to steal.

Thought they would make a tasty meal.

But now I've gotten in a bind.

'Cause Nobody is robbing me blind!

Help!

Your brother,

Polyphemus Cyclops

Athena gasped. It sounded like Mr. Cyclops's brother was planning to munch her hero and his crew!

Hearing the message, a giggle burst from Medusa. Mr. Cyclops frowned at her, and she covered her mouth with both hands, looking like she wished she could recall her laughter. Athena could totally understand why she'd giggled, though. What the magic wind had said about *nobody* was just so silly! What could that part of the message meant?

Hey, wait a minute, thought Athena. Medusa had *giggled!* Just like her fortune had foretold, *nobody*—or at least hearing the word *nobody*—had made her do it.

Suddenly a strange look came over Mr. Cyclops's face. He reached into his pocket and pulled out a little piece of papyrus. It was another Oracle-O fortune. He must've gotten it in a cookie from that basket yesterday too.

"Nobody, my foot," he murmured. His single big eye found Athena across the room. "What is my brother talking about? Your hero is apparently the one robbing him. But who or what is 'nobody'?"

Gulp! Athena was in trouble now. "I don't know exactly, but . . ."

"We'll talk about this later, young lady!" Mr. Cyclops said before she could finish. Then he turned and rushed for the classroom door. "Excuse me, students, I've got a family emergency!" he called back over his shoulder.

"Principal Zeus will send a substitute after I inform him I'll be gone for the rest of the day. So behave!"

After the teacher left, the students all stared at one another. Athena pretended not to notice Poseidon's satisfied smirk. Things were working out better for him than for her right now for sure!

Right away, some of the others in class started cutting up. A few girls began chatting, and some boys, including Poseidon, scooted their desks together to begin a game of javelin football. Medusa went to her desk and started drawing those comics she liked doodling.

Other students kept doing their assignments, though. Aphrodite sidled around the game board map toward Ithaca to see what was going on with Penelope at Odysseus's house.

Meanwhile, Athena peered at the little game board cave that represented where Mr. Cyclops's brother lived.

Somehow she had to rescue her hero! But even with her eyeball up against the cave entrance, it was too dark to see inside. And the opening was so small that she couldn't get her hand in there to pull her hero and his crew out. She put her ear to the opening and heard a faint sound. *Baaa.*

Sheep? *Hmm.* That gave her an idea. Quickly she put her mouth near the cave entrance and called to Odysseus, whispering instructions for an escape plan. Then she straightened. Now all she could do was wait and hope her idea worked.

A few minutes later Principal Zeus entered the classroom. Homer was with him. Back again for another visit, apparently. And this time the author had brought along an artist who was wearing a press badge that said he worked for *Teen Scrollazine.*

"Greetings, students!" Zeus boomed. "I'll be your

substitute for the rest of the hour." He smiled a broad smile and held his arms wide as if expecting applause. Which he got, since students respected him and none would dare offend him. At seven feet tall, with bulging muscles and piercing blue eyes, he was both imposing and intimidating. Wide, flat, golden bracelets encircled both of his wrists, and he wore a thunderbolt belt buckle. Athena often marveled that he was *her* dad!

As everyone dutifully smiled and clapped, the artist whipped out his drawing pad. Seeing this, Zeus's eyes lit up. He turned sideways and struck a pose that showed off his muscles.

Homer studied the game board and then the students while the artist sketched. "So this is where it all began!" he exclaimed with delight. "And you are the very students who guided the events of the Trojan War I wrote about in *The Iliad.* How exciting!"

Athena was excited to see him again too. He was soon to be a published author, after all. And she *lived* to read. Poems, textscrolls—even the advertisements on the back of ambrosia cereal boxes. If it was in print, she would read it. And to think she and some of her friends were going to be actual characters in a published scrollbook! Wow! Even if the Trojan horse had been left out, she couldn't wait to buy a copy and get it autographed at his book signing a week from tomorrow.

Apollo seemed pretty in awe of Homer too, Athena noticed. Made sense. Not only was he the godboy of prophecy, he was also the godboy of poetry. So he appreciated authors and books just like she did.

"So, what are you writing now? I mean, what's your next published scrollbook after *The Iliad* going to be about?" Apollo asked Homer. At the question the author's expression fell, and he mumbled something under his breath that sounded like, "I wish I knew."

The artist's sketch of Zeus was finished, and now Zeus was walking around the far side of the game board, studying it. Seeing this, Homer perked up and hurried over to nudge the artist. "Quick! Maybe you can do an action drawing? With Zeus in the background. And with me in the foreground directing the students to move their heroes around the board? You could make it look like my scrollbook *caused* the events of the Trojan War!"

"The war is over," said Medusa. She'd slipped on her stoneglasses, Athena saw. Otherwise Homer and the artist would've turned to stone. Because that's what happened when mortals dared to gaze at her.

Homer eyed the dozen snakes wriggling around on top of Medusa's head and took a step backward. "I know that. I was just suggesting a re-enactment to illustrate the article in *Teen Scrollazine*. Good advertising, you know?

Mr. Dolos, my publicist, said that some dramatic images in the article would showcase me and my scrollbook."

At the name of his publicist, Medusa's eyes and those of all twelve of her snakes narrowed. Mr. Dolos was also the owner of Be a Hero, of course. He was a wily promoter of people *and* products. And for a short time a while back, he'd tricked Medusa into letting him put a scary-looking version of her head on some shields he'd sold in his store in the Immortal Marketplace.

"Hey! What's happening?" Poseidon demanded suddenly. His eyes were on the game board.

Athena checked it just in time to see a line of sheep running out of Polyphemus's cave. But where was her hero?

"Look! Odysseus and his soldiers tied themselves to the bellies of those sheep to sneak out of Mr. Cyclops's brother's cave. How clever!" she heard someone say.

Hooray! Odysseus had followed her whispered instructions, Athena realized. He and his men had escaped the cave by clinging to the undersides of Polyphemus's sheep as the woolly creatures had trotted outside to graze on the hillsides. Unfortunately, Polyphemus was right behind them. And, even worse, Odysseus had apparently decided to steal the sheep. Argh! She hadn't advised him to do that!

As Odysseus and his men sailed away, he shouted to Polyphemus, "Don't forget what I told you. My name is 'Nobody'!"

Polyphemus gnashed his teeth. Then he called to his giant Cyclops friends for help. "Nobody stole my food! And now he's sailing away with my sheep!" he told them.

His friends just laughed. Because, in their opinions, if *nobody* had stolen Polyphemus's food and his sheep, then what was his problem? Odysseus and his twelve ships made a clean getaway from the island.

By now Zeus was booming with laughter. He always enjoyed a good joke. Athena couldn't help grinning too. She was pretty sure she and her hero had won *that* round against Poseidon. She felt proud of Odysseus for thinking of that Nobody trick all by himself. He must have guessed that when the Cyclops called for help to defeat Nobody, he'd sound silly and his friends would simply ignore him. He'd been right! Smarts like that were what made her hero, well, a hero!

Homer had been watching the whole thing. "Awesome escape plan! Was it yours?" he said, looking at Athena with admiration. She nodded.

"What a scoop! Hold still, you three," the artist instructed Athena, Homer, and Zeus. Zeus immediately stopped laughing and did his muscle pose again. "Mortals will go wild to see all this action," the artist proclaimed as he sketched. "Everyone has always wondered what this game board looked like and how it works." Swiftly he did a drawing of the trio in front of the Hero-ology game board.

Just as the sketch was finished, a gleeful expression came over Homer's face and he looked at Athena. "I just got a scrolltastic idea for my next scrollbook. I'm going to follow you around from now on and write about Odysseus's adventures on his way home to Ithaca!"

Seeing Zeus's raised eyebrows, Homer quickly added, "With Zeus's permission, of course."

"Great idea!" the artist whooped. "This'll be fantastic publicity for your book signing too. So, tell me, what will you title the new scrollbook, Homer?" He paused, his quill pen poised to quote the author's reply.

"I know!" Zeus exclaimed before Homer could speak. "How about *Zeus on the Loose: The King of the*

Gods and Ruler of the Heavens Saves the Day. Or maybe *Zeus's and Odysseus's Excellent Adventure.* Or just *Odyssey Goes . . .* um . . ." He paused, considering how to finish.

Everyone stared. He'd misspoken Odysseus's name in the third, incomplete title. And they all knew Zeus hadn't really been *on* the adventure with Odysseus, so putting his name in the first two titles was a little misleading.

Thinking fast, Athena jumped on that last error. "*Odyssey?* That's perfect, Dad! You just tweaked my hero's name to make up a new word that means 'trip' or 'journey,' right? You're suggesting that Homer could call his sequel *The Odyssey?*" She sent a meaningful glance toward the other students. "Has a ring to it, don't you think?"

They must've caught on that she was trying to smooth over the awkward moment, because they began nodding and smiling. A few even cheered.

"But—" Homer began.

Catching his eye, Athena shook her head in warning. Wasn't it better to accept this title than to be stuck with the earlier ones Zeus had suggested?

Homer took the hint. "Um, yeah, it's catchy . . . I guess."

A broad smile crossed Zeus's face, and he clapped a hand on the author's back. "Thanks, Homie!"

"Ow!" Homer yelped when Zeus's electricity zapped him. But then, seeing that the artist had begun sketching the two of them together, Homer managed a weak but toothy smile.

Just then the lyrebell rang, signaling the end of first period. Athena sent Odysseus a last look of concern. He could still get in plenty of trouble before class tomorrow. But she couldn't stay here and hero-sit him all day. She had to get to her other classes!

Once Athena, Apollo, and Aphrodite left the classroom together, Aphrodite dashed off for her dorm room up on the fourth floor. "I'm going to change out of this hideous outfit," she called with a wave. "See you later!"

Persephone and Artemis came down the hall toward Athena just as she and Apollo reached her locker, and they all stopped to chat. Athena's hand brushed the skirt of her chiton, and she felt something in her pocket. She reached in, found Medusa's fortune, and read it again. She'd stuck it in there earlier, when she'd been in a hurry to help her hero and had forgotten to give the slip back to Medusa.

Now she frowned at it. Hadn't it said something different before? "Hey, look at Medusa's cookie fortune," she told the others. "Before, it said, '*Nobody* will make you giggle.' Now it says, '*Somebody* will make you giggle.'"

"Huh?" Her three companions crowded around to read it together.

"Are you sure you and Medusa just didn't misread it at first?" asked Artemis.

"I don't think so," said Athena.

"You know, I'm not sure I believe in prophecies all that much," Persephone commented.

"Excuse me?" Apollo said in a teasing voice. "I'm trying not to be insulted by that statement."

She grinned at him. "I believe in your prophecies, of course! I only meant the ones in those fortune cookies we got. Mine was so blah. And it brought me bad luck." She pulled the fortune out of her scrollbag and read: "'Your green thumb will not turn brown.'"

"What? Let me see," asked Athena. Persephone held out her fortune so Athena could read it for herself. It *did* say that. "That's weird. I thought it said your thumb *would* turn brown."

Persephone cocked her head. "You know, that's what

I thought at first. And it did turn brown in a way. I accidentally killed some poor unsuspecting zinnias this morning before class."

This was getting even weirder! thought Athena.

"I don't believe in those cookie fortunes either," Artemis said. "Remember mine said I would hit every target? It was wrong. I missed five in a row yesterday for the first time in my life! I think those fortunes brought bad luck too."

Apollo's eyes rounded. "What are you talking about? I saw your fortune. It said you'd *miss* five targets."

"Oh, really?" Artemis dug around in her quiver. She pulled out a torn textscroll, some arrows, a dog leash, and a broken quill pen. Finally she found her crumpled fortune and handed it to him.

Athena peered over his shoulder. "Ye gods! Whoa! She's right! It does say she'll hit every target. Wait, I put

my fortune and Aphrodite's in my scrollbag, I think."
She pulled two slips of papyrus from her bag and
scanned them. Her eyes were wide as she handed one
to Apollo.

He read it aloud. "Aphrodite's says, 'You have great
fashion sense.'"

"See what I mean?" Persephone put in. "Blah.
Because everybody knows that about her."

"So what does yours say?" Artemis asked Athena.

"'An owl, of course,'" Athena admitted.

Her three friends stared at her. Goose bumps rose on
Athena's arms. What was going on here?

"I guess you must've misread it the first time when
you thought it said, '*A horse, of course,*' Persephone
mused slowly.

"Yeah, you're probably right," Athena heard herself
say. For some reason she suddenly actually believed

that to be the case! "Those cookie fortunes got it all wrong. Strange. Usually they're pretty accurate."

"Did you notice what's on the back of this, besides the drawing, I mean?" Apollo held up Medusa's fortune and pointed at the name scrawled at the bottom of it. "It says, 'Cassandra.' And it's printed on papyrus letterhead with the Oracle-O Bakery logo."

"That shop is in the Immortal Marketplace," said Artemis.

"Maybe we should go there and investigate," Athena suggested. "Find out who this Cassandra is and why she's sending us these crazy fortunes!"

5

The Oracle-O Bakery

Cassandra

As soon as Cassandra walked downstairs from her bedroom to work in the bakery Saturday morning, she saw it. The big half-built carousel beyond the bakery's front door that hadn't been there the night before. It was pretty hard to miss, since it stood right in the middle of the IM's atrium.

The carousel was twenty feet tall and its platform was

three rows wide, with the highest row toward its center. But it wasn't painted or decorated yet, and there weren't any animals or chariots to ride.

Helenus shook his head. "Whoa! I didn't see this coming."

Cassandra hesitated. She *had* foreseen it. She'd even put the idea for the carousel into a fortune for Zeus. But Helenus didn't know anything about that. She and Andromache hadn't known how Homer and the carousel fit together when Cassandra had written her fortunes either.

"Well, even the very best of oracles can't know *everything* ahead of time," she told her brother. Though she was annoyed that everyone thought his prophecies were way better than hers, that wasn't his fault, so she tried not to be mean about it. "It's pretty much random what parts of the future can be seen."

"True," Helenus agreed readily.

Laodice had been behind the counter, ready for the store's first customers. But now she moved to just inside the glass door, craning her neck to see what was going on outside. "Look! Mom's out there. With Zeus!" she announced in an excited voice. It wasn't every day the King of the Gods and Ruler of the Heavens came to the IM.

Cassandra went to the storefront window and studied the big crowd that had gathered around the carousel. "Why is he hanging out with Mom?"

"And who's that mortal guy with spiky blue hair talking to Zeus and her?" Helenus asked. Before anyone could guess, Helenus noticed something that interested him even more. "Hey! There's Ares—the godboy of war! Awesome." He took off to go talk to him.

"Ooh!" said Laodice. "And that hunky Poseidon's out

there too! And Heracles and Pan! They're all even cuter than their pictures in *Teen Scrollazine*," she said, sounding thrilled. She raced back to the counter, grabbed the hand mirror she kept underneath it, and primped her hair. After checking her makeup, too, she made a dash for the door like their brother just had.

Cassandra went after her, planning to follow. She wanted to know exactly what was going on. But as the two girls pushed out into the atrium, Laodice exclaimed, "Wow, look! Those four mega-popular goddessgirls are here too!"

Cassandra froze. She could see the goddessgirls now. Athena, Aphrodite, Persephone, and Artemis were easy to spot. Even among a crowd of other amazing immortals, they stood out. They were fantastically beautiful! Zeus's wedding had been so busy that she hadn't gotten to talk to them. And even though she had often imagined telling Athena and Aphrodite how mad she was at them if she got the chance, she suddenly panicked. She wasn't up for a confrontation right now.

Her heart started beating faster. They must *not* see her! Quickly she ducked back inside the shop and dropped to a crouch, out of view behind the shelf of cookies just inside the front door. Then she peeked up over the shelf to survey the mob around the carousel while she tried to calm herself. It wasn't unusual for immortals to come here to the IM. But she'd never seen this many at once.

As Cassandra watched the four goddessgirls, Persephone wandered off to talk to a boy. She couldn't see his face from the bakery, but it was probably Hades. The rumor was that they liked each other.

All of a sudden, Athena turned her head in the store's direction. The big Oracle-O Bakery sign painted on the front window seemed to have caught her eye. She nudged

Aphrodite and Artemis, who were on either side of her, and then pointed at the bakery. The girls looked toward it and then over at Zeus. Seeming to decide they wouldn't be needed for a while, they headed for the store.

"Yikes!" Cassandra almost had a heart attack. Staying hunkered down so they wouldn't notice her, she began backing away from the door. It had been one thing to send troublemaking fortunes to them and to gossip about them with her friend Andromache. The possibility of actually having to face them after what she'd done made her feel a little embarrassed and scared.

Had they guessed that she'd sent the fortunes? Were they mad? Had they come here to pay *her* back? Would they rat her out to Zeus? He could obliterate the entire IM with a thunderbolt if he wanted to.

When the bell on the door tinkled, Cassandra ducked behind the store check-out counter to hide. She scrunched down to sit on the floor, wrapping both arms around her bent knees. Maybe the goddessgirls would just go away if no one came to help them. As they came inside, she listened to them talking among themselves.

"Mmm," one of them said. "This store smells *sooo* good."

"If I worked in a bakery, I'd be as big as the Academy because I wouldn't be able to resist sampling all these sweets," said another of the goddessgirls.

"My dogs would go crazy in here," said a third voice, which had to be Artemis's. Everyone knew she had three hounds that she adored.

"Hello?" one of them called out in a loud voice. "Anyone here?"

The bell on the door tinkled again as someone new came into the store.

"Welcome!" said two familiar voices, one high and one low. Laodice and Helenus! They must've seen the goddessgirls heading for the store and followed them in, Cassandra realized.

"We're looking for the fortune-teller. The one who puts fortunes into your cookies, I mean," said one of the goddessgirls. Cassandra's intuition, which was almost as good as her fortune-telling skills, told her that it was probably Athena.

"I do all the Oracle-O fortunes," Helenus told them, sounding thrilled to meet the goddesses.

"Oh! Well, we're looking for someone named Cassandra, though," Athena went on. "Because we got these fortunes."

Cassandra peeked out around the edge of the counter a little and saw Athena show him a small slip of papyrus. Helenus and Laodice frowned at it.

"Where did you get this?" Helenus demanded, sounding upset now.

"Only the spoken fortunes are meant to go to Mount Olympus Academy," Laodice added. "Written fortunes go to Earth. There must've been some mix-up."

"So no one named Cassandra works here?" a goddess-girl with beautiful blue eyes and golden hair asked. Aphrodite, Cassandra figured.

Just then Laodice came over to the counter. She almost tripped over Cassandra as she went to step behind it. "What are you doing down there?" she exclaimed.

"Shhh," hissed Cassandra, putting a finger to her lips. But it was too late.

Suddenly a girl with long, wavy brown hair leaned over the counter to see what Laodice was looking at. It was Athena. Her skin glittered softly as her intelligent blue-gray eyes studied Cassandra. "Hi," she said.

"Hi," Cassandra replied in a squeaky voice. She uncurled and jumped to her feet. "Were you looking for me? I'm Cassandra." Then she added, "I was just getting a box." Reaching down, she grabbed an empty cookie box at random from some shelves behind the counter and then set it on the countertop so she wouldn't look like a liar.

"Did you write these?" asked Athena. She held out three of the papyrus slips that Cassandra had put into the cookies she'd given Hermes two days ago to take to MOA. It had seemed like a good idea at the time. But now Cassandra wasn't so sure. Although, Athena looked more puzzled than angry.

Cassandra nodded. She gave the fortunes a cursory glance, her mouth twisting when she saw the words on them. Of course the fortunes had changed from the way she'd originally written them. Because of the curse, any fortune she wrote down changed after it was pulled from a cookie and read. It could take only minutes or as long as a day, but eventually her words would rearrange themselves to make her appear a liar. Or at least a bad fortune-teller!

Even if she put a spoken fortune into a cookie like Helenus did, within a day after the cookie was opened and its fortune spoken, the recipient would remember her words all wrong.

"I'm really sorry for any trouble or anguish those fortunes may have caused," Laodice told Athena, looking worried. "Please accept our apologies."

Cassandra knew that what she had done could reflect badly on the store, and now she wished she'd never done it. Andromache claimed that immortals lived to make life difficult for mortals. What would her family do if they didn't have the store? Immortals had the power to take what little mortals had completely away from them. They could do anything they wanted!

"It was all my idea. Please don't make trouble for my family, okay?" Cassandra said anxiously.

"We're not mad," Aphrodite assured her, coming over. "We just want you to know that your fortunes weren't accurate."

The golden-haired goddessgirl, who was dressed all in pink, was as dazzling as Cassandra remembered from Zeus and Hera's wedding. So dazzling that for a minute Cassandra couldn't reply. Then finally she found her tongue. "You mean they didn't come true? You didn't lose your fashion sense for a while?" she challenged Aphrodite.

"Um," said Aphrodite. "But that's not what your fortune said."

Cassandra turned to Athena. "You didn't say 'A horse, of course'?"

"Well," Athena said uncertainly.

"So my fortunes weren't true? They were completely

wrong?" Cassandra asked. All three of the goddessgirls in the shop stared at her, looking confused.

Their confusion told her everything she needed to know. Her fortunes *had* come true. But then the slips had changed to make these goddessgirls think they hadn't. Just like with the Trojan horse. All because of the curse. The curse put on her by that godboy . . .

Apollo! At the very second she thought his name, the bell on the door tinkled again. And he walked right into the store! Cassandra's breath caught and her eyes narrowed. *Grrr.*

Then her eyes flicked back to the goddessgirls again. "The fortunes you found in those cookies *did* come true. And their accuracy wasn't a fluke," she insisted. But even as she said this, she knew that the curse had defeated her. There was no way they'd believe her when the "proof" of her prophecies' falseness was printed right there on those magically altered little slips of papyrus.

Cassandra felt ready to explode. But really, what had she expected? She'd wanted to stir up a little trouble for Athena, Aphrodite, Apollo, and their friends. And she had. Enough to bring them in here to make trouble for *her*, unfortunately!

The only fortune that was truly important, though, was the one she'd given Zeus. Everybody knew he was impulsive. And he'd acted on the carousel fortune, just as she and Andromache had hoped. They hadn't guessed he would actually build a carousel here in the IM. Still, Cassandra had a feeling that the carousel somehow held the key to fully executing their payback plan!

"Hey! We're sorry about the dud fortunes," Helenus said to the immortals. He glared at Cassandra.

"Why don't you all look around the store?" Laodice

coaxed their visitors in a cheerful voice. "What kind of cookies are your favorites? Pick some out. No charge."

"Well, thanks," said Athena. "I'll take some for my dad. He's got a real sweet tooth." As sorry as Cassandra felt for herself, she was glad that good old Laodice had succeeded in covering for her by distracting the goddessgirls.

Meanwhile Helenus fawned over Apollo, asking him questions about MOA and archery and war-related stuff. Chastened, Cassandra worked the counter, busying herself with filling cookie orders and hoping these immortals would all leave soon.

After a few minutes of listening to the goddessgirls, though, she had to admit they didn't seem as bad as Andromache claimed they were. They weren't being rude to her sister and brother or anything. In fact, they were being very polite.

Then, while dropping a handful of coconut ambrosia bites into a papyrus bag, Cassandra smelled peppermints. Leaving the bag on the counter, she grabbed a quill pen and some papyrus and started writing.

As she did, she felt Apollo glance her way. Eyeing her curiously, he left Helenus talking to Artemis and came over to the counter. "Hi. Do I know you? You look familiar," he told her.

Cassandra gazed at him wordlessly. Then she slid the fortune she'd just written across the counter to him. It read: *You will meet someone who looks familiar.*

Looking surprised and impressed, the dark-haired godboy studied her even more closely. "Nice work. But for a fortune it's kind of general, isn't it?"

"Yeah, I suppose." Cassandra wadded up the fortune and tossed it away. "You're right, though. We *have* met before. Twice, actually."

He stared at her even harder. Then suddenly his brows rose. "Yeah! I remember now. You were my bridesmaid at Zeus and Hera's wedding."

He was right, though they hadn't said more than two words to each other at the busy wedding. He'd chosen her to accompany him down the aisle by drawing her name from a helmet filled with names of girls who were dying to be chosen as bridesmaids. She'd known he was going to pick her name, but of course nobody had believed her when she'd told them so. Anyway, that wasn't the meeting she'd wanted him to remember. Had he completely forgotten their earlier meeting in the temple? And his curse?

He cocked his head, studying her. "Your hair was curly back then."

She shrugged. "I wanted it to have more waves and volume, so I tried a body wave for the wedding. Usually my hair is straight, though, like now."

"Well, I think it looks good the way it is," Apollo said, to her surprise. He immediately blushed.

"Uh, thanks." She sort of wished he wouldn't be nice to her like this. It made it harder for her to dislike him.

"So, you wrote those fortunes we got," Apollo mused. "What did mine mean? *'Your curse you should reverse'*?"

"Are you sure that's what it said?" she asked, surprised that he'd recalled it correctly. By now most other people would have gotten it all mixed up.

He nodded. Then he straightened, a strange look coming over his face. "Can I borrow your pen?" he asked.

When she shrugged, he took her pen and a piece of papyrus and wrote something. She watched him, trying not to notice how cute he was with his wavy black hair and dark eyes.

As he finished writing, her mom burst into the store, her eyes twinkling with excitement. "I have amazing news! Zeus has just offered to help us put on a fantastic event in the store. There'll be carousel rides, food and drink, and more. And best of all, an author named Homer will autograph his new scrollbook, *The Iliad*!"

So that's what Homer's book was called. In her version of it, Cassandra hadn't seen the title in her vision.

Just then Apollo pushed the papyrus he'd scribbled on across the counter toward Cassandra. She read it silently. *Your mother will have amazing news.*

Cassandra lifted an eyebrow at him, and then repeated his words to her. "For a fortune it's kind of general, isn't it?"

When Apollo burst out laughing, she couldn't help giggling a little too. Catching Athena's eye, she waved her closer and handed her the bag of coconut ambrosia bites.

"Thanks! My dad's going to be absolutely *thunderstruck* when he sees these," said Athena.

Since Zeus was often known to hurl thunderbolts,

Cassandra grinned at her humorous use of "thunder-struck." She had planned to be rude to these immortals if she ever got the chance. Especially to the Three A's. But now she was kind of in awe of them. Because although they didn't have to treat her and her family as equals, they were. And they were actually pretty funny. And nice. And up close, immortals simply inspired awe!

Still, she couldn't forgive some things. As Athena and her friends talked to Helenus and Laodice a bit longer, Cassandra turned back to Apollo. "You really don't remember the other time we met?" she asked.

He looked at her blankly. Which made her kind of mad, actually. How could he *not* remember the curse that had ruined her life, even if they had only been little kids at the time?

Before she could remind him of that first meeting, the doorbell tinkled again and Andromache came in. Her friend sent her a smile, then glared at the immortals big-time. Behind their backs, though, Cassandra noticed.

She looked down at the fortune she'd given Apollo only ten minutes ago. Predictably, it now read: *You will* not *meet someone who looks familiar.*

Tears of frustration welled in her eyes, and she wadded the paper into a ball. "Um, I have to go," she told him abruptly. Without another word she rushed into the back office.

Andromache followed her. "Awww. You look upset," she told Cassandra. Her eyes were full of sympathy. "Having to be nice to those rotten immortals just so your family wouldn't get mad at you was awful, huh? That must've been awful." Putting an arm around her, Andromache gave Cassandra a comforting hug.

Cassandra knew that Andromache expected her to agree that the immortals were awful. But when she tried to summon the angry feelings she'd nurtured for so long against all the immortals—especially Apollo—she just couldn't do it. Because now that she'd met some of them, they didn't really seem that bad. It was all so confusing.

Out in the shop the bell tinkled yet again. Andromache peeked into the bakery from the office. "Good. They're gone. Those immortals think they're such hot stuff. Always messing in mortal business. Stuck-up troublemakers, that's what they are. Why did they come into the store anyway? For free cookies?" Her eyes gleamed with curiosity.

Cassandra cringed at Andromache's expression of ill will toward the immortals. Is that what she had sounded like too, up until today? "It's okay. I guess I sort of invited them in a way," she admitted. She plopped down at the office desk, picked up a quill pen, and twirled it in her fingers.

Andromache's mouth dropped open. "Why would you do that? They're your enemies! They're the reason we had to leave Troy and come here!"

Andromache had had a crush on Cassandra's oldest brother, Hector, before the war. In Cassandra's opinion that was the whole reason Andromache resented the immortals so much. She probably figured that, if not for the Trojan War, Hector would still be around and in like with her.

"Having those immortals invade this bakery is almost like inviting the Trojan horse through the gates of Troy," Andromache went on.

At the mention of the Trojan horse, Cassandra stiffened. Andromache was right. Those immortals had caused massive trouble for her and her family. For *all* of Troy. What had she been thinking, having fun with them?

"I didn't *invite* them exactly," she said. "I just meant they came here because of those payback fortunes we sent."

Andromache folded her arms. "So did you ask them to explain the trouble they caused us? And did Apollo apologize for the curse? Did Athena say she was sorry about the Trojan horse? And Aphrodite? Did she say she felt bad about making Paris fall in love with Helen in the first place?"

"Well, no," Cassandra admitted. "Those things never came up."

Suddenly she smelled lemons. It was a scent that rarely came to her with predictions. Lemon fortunes were usually a bit sour, but they never came true unless the people they were intended for found out about them. Automatically Cassandra grabbed the nearest piece of papyrus. It was some of the yellow polka-dot kind they used to make labels for the trays of cookies on the store shelves. She began to write. When she finished, Andromache looked at what she'd written.

Athena's horse will crack itself up.

Aphrodite will be embarrassed by really baaad makeup.

Apollo will stand speechless in the middle of chaos.

"Ha! Those are fun," said Andromache. "Write some more."

After having met the immortals, Cassandra felt kind of bad that these fortunes seemed so mean. But she couldn't help the predictions that came to her, and the immortals would never know about them. So no harm done, right? Besides, she enjoyed making Andromache laugh. As the smell of lemon came again, she put pen to papyrus.

6

The Carousel

Cassandra

A DOZEN CHOCOLATE NUT CRUNCH THUNDER-
bolts," boomed a powerful voice. "With sprinkles." It
was Monday morning, and Zeus—King of the Gods and
Ruler of the Heavens—was standing in the Oracle-O
Bakery, already placing his *second* cookie order of the day.

*Athena hadn't been kidding about him having a sweet
tooth!* thought Cassandra as she watched from the

bakery kitchen. From her current spot she could see out to the counter, where Laodice and Helenus were helping Zeus, and beyond them into the store.

"Fortunes spoken or written?" Helenus asked Zeus in an awe-filled tone.

"Spoken, of course," said Zeus in a voice that crackled with authority.

"Certainly," said Laodice, shooting their brother a questioning glance. *Helenus must be nervous,* thought Cassandra. Why else would he have asked Zeus that? Immortals *always* got Helenus's magic spoken fortunes. Except for the ones Cassandra herself sent to MOA without permission last week.

Cassandra wasn't the only one watching Zeus buy cookies. The construction in the scrollbook shop next door was now finished. While doing the cleanup, the workers kept peeking into the bakery through the open archway that connected the two stores, so they could stare in wonderment at the bakery's powerful customer.

A crowd had gathered out in the IM atrium too, to peer through the bakery's front windows. The King of the Gods was a busy guy and didn't come here often, so immortals and mortals alike were naturally curious!

Once word got around that Zeus had bought thunderbolt cookies, Cassandra figured other customers would also want to order them. So she started making more of the chocolate nut crunch cookie dough.

As she kneaded a big ball of dough in the bakery kitchen, she watched her sister choose twelve perfect thunderbolt-shaped chocolate nut crunch Oracle-O cookies and put them into a tissue-lined white box. They all had Helenus's fortunes inside them, of course. Not Cassandra's.

She couldn't help noticing that Laodice's hands

shook a little as she handed the cookies over to Zeus. Probably afraid of accidentally getting zapped by the tiny sparks that ran up and down his muscled arms, thought Cassandra. Zeus lit up with excitement just like a little kid as he took the box. Unable to wait he opened it on his way out and began munching a thunderbolt before he'd even left the store.

"You have an electric personality!" the cookie told him as he pushed open the door.

Cassandra rolled her eyes. That was no fortune. By giving him "prophecies" like that, Helenus was just stroking Zeus's ego like their mom had asked him to. Understandably, Hecuba didn't want anything to go wrong during Zeus's visit! Especially the upcoming author event the King of the Gods had helped plan.

Elaborate invitations had gone out this morning to a guest list that included royalty, immortals, and the greatest heroes on Earth. A big announcement had also been placed in the *Greekly Weekly News* to invite mortals to the bakery and scrollbook shop this coming Saturday. It was going to be tons of fun, with Zeus and Homer as the star attractions.

Even now Cassandra's mom was out in front of the bakery in the atrium with the goddessgirl Pheme and the *Teen Scrollazine* artist. Pheme was going to include an "Events Too Amazing to Miss" article about the author book signing party in her gossip column. Her mom had bartered with the artist, trading cookies for the painting of a new bakery sign with the name she'd decided on earlier. It was already up and now read, ORACLE-O BAKERY AND SCROLLBOOKS. Just this morning her mom had asked him to add a tagline that read: *Cookies so good, the King of the Gods shops here!*

Beyond the bakery storefront, a big mob of people milled around the atrium. Since the storeowners and their families needed extra time to prepare for the big event, IM school had been canceled for the week. So there were lots of IM kids hanging out, mostly watching the MOA students work their magic.

The MOA-ers had come back this morning to set up the carousel and had bought tons of supplies from different stores in the Immortal Marketplace. Because of them, business was booming for everyone!

Rumor had it that after the author party, the carousel that was being built would become a permanent attraction in the atrium. Right now the immortals were creating carousel animals big enough to ride on.

Cassandra wanted to go watch the students' progress too. But she was needed in the store. With so many people in the IM, the bakery's sales were the best they'd ever been. And now that word had gotten around about Zeus's fondness for their cookies, even more people were coming into the store. The bell tinkled constantly. If this kept up, and with the bookshop to run too, the family was going to have to hire some help.

Catching her eye, Cassandra's mom gestured through the window to her to come outside the store. "Watch the oven, okay?" Cassandra told her sister and brother as she passed them. Then she pushed out the front door and went to see what their mom wanted.

"Will you take some cookies out into the atrium and offer them to the MOA students working on the carousel?" Hecuba asked her. "It'll be great publicity if everyone sees immortals enjoying them."

It was a good idea, but Cassandra had mixed feelings about hanging out with immortals. "I don't know, Mom. Laodice and Helenus won't be able to handle things inside on their own, so I'm not sure—"

"I'll help them," a voice offered. Cassandra looked

over her shoulder to see that Andromache had come along.

"Andromache! You're such a dear," Hecuba told her, giving her a quick hug. The girl beamed, obviously pleased. The reason she lived here in the IM with her aunt and uncle was that her parents traveled a lot. But her aunt and uncle already had four kids of their own and were really into their Magical Wagical store business, so they didn't have much time for Andromache. She probably didn't get many hugs, except the ones Cassandra and her mom gave her, thought Cassandra.

"You've got a wonderful touch with baking," Hecuba went on.

Andromache's smile grew even wider. "I can stay all day."

As the two girls hurried back inside the bakery, Cassandra asked, "Are you sure you want to help? You wouldn't rather laze around this week, at least in the afternoons while there's no school?"

"Not a bit. I know your mom has to keep those immortals happy. Besides, if you circulate among them, it could be a good opportunity to overhear something that'll help us get going on more payback." Before Cassandra could voice a protest, Andromache went on. "Anyway, you know I love the bakery. And with school out, my cousins are helping at the magic store, so I'm free."

Cassandra nodded, knowing it was true. Andromache enjoyed cooking and kitchens way more than she did the magic store stuff. In fact, she loved baking as much as Cassandra loved to read!

As they entered the kitchen area, Cassandra sniffed the air. "Uh-oh! I smell almost-burning cookies!" The girls dashed over just in time to save the trays she'd left in the oven.

"Phew! That was close," said Cassandra. "I guess Laodice and Helenus were too busy to notice the whole place was about to burn down."

"A slight exaggeration," Andromache teased. She got busy dropping more dough onto cookie sheets. When Cassandra continued to stand there, her friend glanced over at her and said, "You'd better get going, huh? I'll take care of things here. See you later?"

Cassandra grinned. Then she whipped off her apron and tossed it to Andromache. "Deal!"

After leaving the kitchen, Cassandra grabbed one of the fancy platters with the store logo and filled it with an assortment of spoken-fortune Oracle-O cookies from the store's bins. Then she headed for the carousel.

"Want a cookie?" she asked the first immortal boy she saw. Eyes the color of purple grapes flicked her way. It was the godboy Dionysus. No other godboy had eyes that unusual color, as far as she knew.

"Can you tell what this is?" he asked her. He gestured with one hand to the animal he was creating on the carousel and took a cookie with his other hand.

"A leopard," she said with certainty.

"Awesome," he told her, seeming relieved. "I can act, but I'm not much of an artist. So I'm glad you can tell what it's supposed to be!"

"Don't be so modest about your artistic skills. Your leopard looks pretty amazing," she encouraged. The *Teen Scrollazine* artist must've thought so too. He'd been roaming around the carousel, sketching immortals. Now he paused to make a drawing of Dionysus painting more spots on the leopard.

Cassandra gave away more cookies as she watched the carousel being constructed. Some animals, like Dionysus's, were further along than others. She could tell from the long ears and the braying sounds Hephaestus's animal was starting to make that Hephaestus was crafting a donkey. And she could also see that Poseidon was creating a dolphin leaping from a wave. Artemis was making a white golden-horned deer pulling a chariot, and Pan was chiseling a sheep with carved swirls on its sides to represent wool.

She paused to watch Aphrodite. The goddessgirl waved her hand in the air, making an S shape. Then she said:

> "*Long slim neck.*
> *Feathers white.*
> *Make a swan*
> *That will delight!*"

A white swan that was taller than the goddessgirl herself began to take shape on the carousel. Aphrodite walked all around it, giving it a critical once-over. It looked perfect to Cassandra but must not have to Aphrodite, because she began saying additional spells to make it look even more graceful and lifelike.

Persephone was on a ladder, magically carving swags of flowers around the bottom edge of the carousel's pointed roof. And another goddessgirl was busily flitting around, painting the carousel with all the colors of the rainbow.

Athena was helping Heracles with what looked to be a lion. He'd taken off his lion cape and was using it as a guide for the face of his animal ride.

Cassandra couldn't tell what Athena was making. Since the goddessgirl had stopped to help Heracles with his lion, her animal wasn't very far along. It was probably going to be an owl, though, because everyone knew that was her favorite animal—the one she identified with the most. But why had she given her owl four furry legs? Cassandra wondered. Where were its feathers?

"Hey, can I have one of those?" asked a boy's voice from behind her.

Cassandra recognized that voice. *Apollo!* She turned around, unable to stop herself from smiling at him. "You lucked out, because I just have one left." She held the tray out to him balanced on one hand, and he snatched the last cookie.

Dropping the tray to her side, she walked in a circle around the animal he was creating. "A raven?" she guessed.

He smiled, his brown eyes twinkling. "Got it in one. I'm glad you didn't say 'crow,' though. Or 'magpie.'"

He unwrapped the spoken-fortune cookie. "You will have an enjoyable treat," it told him. Grinning, he popped the cookie into his mouth. "Mmm. Totally accurate," he said.

"I didn't write that prophecy," she said quickly. It was one of Helenus's of course. She didn't want Apollo to think she'd ever come up with such a generic fortune! When he didn't reply, she shifted from one foot to the other, suddenly feeling a little shy and not knowing what else to say. "Okay, well . . . guess I'd better go." She took a step in the direction of the bakery.

Apollo pulled a slip of papyrus from the pocket of his tunic and held it out to her. It was the payback fortune she'd written. It had originally said: *Your curse you should reverse.* Only, now it read: *Your curse you won't reverse.*

"Explain," he said.

Whoa! She looked at him warily. He actually seemed to get it that the fortunes were changing on their own. Others always assumed that the altered fortunes were what she'd originally written, and then would decide that her prophecies must be mistakes or lies. Did his ability to see that her fortune had actually changed itself have something to do with him being the godboy of prophecy? Or else the creator of the curse?

"Within one day after someone reads a fortune I write, they remember it all wrong," she told him bluntly. "Plus the words on the fortune actually change to say something different from what I originally wrote."

His eyes widened. "What about when you speak a fortune?"

"Same thing. It can take anywhere from a few minutes to a day for anyone who hears it to remember it wrong. But they always do." Suddenly the long years of frustration at prophesying truths that were never believed got the better of her. "And it's your fault!" she exclaimed.

Apollo's head drew back in surprise. "What? No way!"

"Yes, way," she insisted. "You really don't remember

me from that first time we met? Seven years ago, before Zeus and Hera's wedding?"

"Huh?"

"I was five years old. My family was on vacation, temple-touring. You were in a temple we visited, all by yourself and in a grumpy mood. I asked you why you were hanging around all alone, and you said it was your temple so you had every right to be there. I said it wasn't yours, and—"

"It wasn't," he said, seeming to believe her. "I guess I just *wished* it was my temple. After all, I *was* pretty young then too. I must've been six years old. I remember that some of the other immortals in my neighborhood who already had temples dedicated to them used to tease me about not having one. In fact, I didn't get my own till this year, when Zeus awarded it to me."

So she'd been right that it wasn't his temple that long

ago day. Still, she didn't rub it in now. His explanation made it a little easier to understand why he'd lashed out at her back then. He'd been frustrated because of the teasing. She knew that feeling too! From being teased about her prophecies. It could sometimes make you act in ways you weren't proud of later.

"What happened," she went on, "was, we got into an argument, and you wound up putting a curse on me. And ever since then no one has believed a single word I prophesy."

Apollo's eyes bugged as he stared at her. "Are you joking? I don't remember any of that."

"Well, it's true," she said. When she looked away from him, her gaze happened to fall on Athena again. She was much further along on her animal ride than she had been just minutes ago. Magical spells had given her animal a firm belly and a long strong column of a neck in addition to four legs. *Huh?* This was no owl! As Cassandra watched, Athena started working on her animal's head.

Apollo was saying something, but her attention was riveted on Athena now. "I figured she would make an owl ride," she murmured with growing horror. "But that looks like . . ."

Before Cassandra could finish her sentence, Athena cast one last spell to create her animal's head. Presto! It now had a long muzzle, flared nostrils, pointed ears, and a flowing mane!

"Excuse me," said a voice. It was the *Teen Scrollazine* artist. "Can I get a sketch of you with Athena and her Trojan horse?" he asked Cassandra as he approached. "For the article."

Cassandra froze. She'd been right to feel alarmed. This wasn't just any horse. It was an exact replica of that dastardly *Trojan* horse!

Oh, no! How could Athena do this to her? Seeing that horse was like a slap in the face. Not only would it remind everyone of the humiliating defeat of her countrymen, but it was also going to remind them of Cassandra's biggest failure at fortune-telling ever!

"Cassandra?" Apollo said. He spoke in an insistent tone that told her he'd been trying to get her attention for a while.

But she wouldn't look at him. Keeping her eyes down, she backed away from him, the artist, and the carousel. Then she raced back to the bakery. As she burst into the kitchen, she breathlessly blurted to her friend Andromache, "Athena's making a Trojan horse on the carousel!"

"What!" exclaimed Andromache, whirling around in dismay. The color drained from her face, but then her expression turned fierce. "She'll be sorry," she vowed.

"What do you mean?" Cassandra asked. She was a bit alarmed at Andromache's response. As much as she disliked what Athena had done, she was beginning to think that exacting revenge was not a good cure for her frustration. It usually just made her feel worse.

Andromache went over to the office desk and picked up a copy of the *Greekly Weekly News* that was lying there. "There's an article in here about Athena and her so-called hero, Odysseus. Seems that in her Hero-ology class she's got the assignment of trying to get him back home to Ithaca. It's really important to her—and to her grade, apparently, which is what that brainster really cares about."

"So?" Cassandra asked blankly. She took the news-scroll and scanned the short article Andromache had pointed out. It told how the immortal students moved little statues if their heroes around on a game board, causing things to happen to the heroes in real life. Which was kind of cool, actually. Though probably a little scary for the heroes!

"So we'll ruin things for her," suggested Andromache, who was pacing now and steaming mad. "Make her look bad. And Aphrodite, too, since she's helping Athena with Odysseus's family."

"Huh? How? What do you mean?" asked Cassandra.

Andromache came to a stop and leaned toward her. "We'll stop Athena's hero, Odysseus, from getting to Ithaca. She'll get a bad grade for sure. The ultimate payback, in her case. I think it's what that carousel fortune you wrote for Zeus must've meant us to do all along. Because it got Homer and the immortals here and gave me the idea, right?"

"What idea? I still don't get it. I mean, even if we wanted to, we can't mess things up on the Hero-ology game board this article mentions. Because we can't go to MOA."

Andromache paused, thinking. Then something—or someone—caught her eye. "But we know someone who can."

Cassandra followed her gaze to see Homer, who was posing for the *Teen Scrollazine* artist in front of Athena's horse. Hurriedly Cassandra looked away again, not wanting to see that dumb horse.

"You can just make up a few fortunes with troubles for Odysseus. And I'll trick that author guy, Homer, into giving the fortunes to the statue of Odysseus on the game board at MOA," said Andromache.

What she said kind of bugged Cassandra. She'd thought Andromache had more faith in her prophecies. "I don't just make them up," she replied. "They have to come to me."

Andromache just shrugged and rushed on. "If we tell Homer that the new fortunes will make Odysseus's adventures more exciting, I think he'll do what we want!"

Wow! Andromache was so good at revenge ideas that Ms. Nemesis—the world-famous Revenge-ology teacher at MOA—could probably take lessons from her! thought Cassandra. She knew if she said the word, Andromache could deliver on her vow for revenge. But something held her back.

"I don't know. I'm not sure we . . . ," Cassandra began uncertainly.

"Cassandra?" Her mom came into the kitchen, smiling. And Homer was with her. Neither of them seemed to notice that anything was wrong. "Andromache is happy on her own in the kitchen," her mom said with a grateful glance at the girl. "And I know how much you enjoy reading and want to work in the scrollbook shop," she said to Cassandra. "So how about if you assist Homer for the rest of the week in getting ready for his scrollbook event?"

"Sure," Cassandra said quickly. She'd rather do bookstore stuff than work in the bakery any day. She was a little worried about what Andromache might do when she wasn't around, however. But without any fortunes, Andromache would have to give up on her payback plan, right? Cassandra could just say she couldn't get into the mental zone to think of any prophecies.

"Cool!" said Homer, smiling at her. "Okay, assistant. Let's get to work."

Snap! He unfurled a scroll he was holding that was so long, it reached all the way to the floor. "Let's go over my to-do list. Number one: At my book signing I will require a dozen quill pens, lined up just so, all perfectly sharp.

Number two: I'll need a chair to sit in—not too hard, not too soft. And it has to be blue, my lucky color. Number three . . ."

Cassandra gulped. Were authors always so demanding? What had she gotten herself into?

7

Odysseus

Athena

MR. CYCLOPS TAPPED THE TOE OF ONE OF HIS

large sandaled feet in irritation. He was sitting at his desk

in Hero-ology on Tuesday morning, and the single big

eye in the center of his forehead was gazing sternly at

Athena. "I don't appreciate your hero Odysseus's making

trouble on my family's island. Stealing food and sheep

from my brother? Is that proper hero behavior?"

Athena shook her head from side to side, her long brown hair swaying. This was so embarrassing. Everyone in class could hear the scolding. Including Homer, who was right beside her, listening in and taking notes on the blank scroll he was holding. Would this conversation go into his new book, *The Odyssey*? She hoped not!

Unlike the way she was feeling right now, *he* looked pretty thrilled. Thanks to the promotion being done by Homer's publicist and Pheme, Odysseus's adventures were becoming big news at MOA, and down on Earth, too.

All this recent hero-caused trouble would be great publicity for Homer's book signing this weekend. But it might not be good for her grade if she couldn't get Odysseus safely home soon.

"However," her teacher admitted, "Polyphemus wasn't entirely blameless. He did try to capture your hero and his men and eat them for dinner, after all. So I'll let it go this time. We'll consider Odysseus's actions an eye for an eye."

"Thanks, Mr. Cyclops," Athena said gratefully. "That's really fair-minded of you. Oh, and I meant to tell you that I made sure Odysseus received a leather bag that contains all the winds that could otherwise blow against his ship and slow him down. Since only the winds that favor his voyage are left on earth right now, he should have smooth sailing from here on out."

The teacher nodded. "Excellent."

After Mr. Cyclops dismissed her, Athena headed for the game board. Now that she'd finished building her horse on the carousel in the Immortal Marketplace, she was back in classes each morning for the rest of the week. She and the other immortals on the project still had to paint their animals and help decorate the carousel itself, though. So they would be returning to the Marketplace every afternoon until the project was complete.

If she had the choice, she'd really rather stay here and watch over Odysseus. She was determined to get him back to his family in Ithaca as swiftly as possible. It wouldn't be easy. That guy had a mind of his own! And some people were out to make trouble for him. She darted a glance in Poseidon's direction.

Even now that drippy godboy was having a conversation with a six-headed sea monster named Scylla who was peering out of the Mediterranean Sea on the game board map. Athena wished she could listen in. However, it wouldn't do her any good to eavesdrop on whatever disasters they might be plotting for Odysseus's future. Because, unlike Poseidon, she didn't speak sea monster!

"So let me get this straight," Homer said while trailing her around the edge of the game board. "Odysseus tricked Polyphemus, a three-eyed Cyclops."

"One-eyed," Athena corrected.

Homer scribbled a quick notation on his scroll. "Oh, yes. That's right. Then he and his men left the cave after tying themselves to the underbellies of some goats?"

"Sheep," Athena corrected. Honestly, he made as many mistakes as Pheme! He needed to hire a fact-checker! Oh, wait. He had a fact-checker. One who was working for free. *Her!*

Homer did another scratch-out, then continued reading aloud what he'd written. "'Once Odysseus was back on board his ship, he tricked Polyphemus again, telling him that his name was Nobody. Which led Polyphemus to start yelling that "Nobody" was stealing from him, which caused the other Cyclops to laugh at him instead of help him out.'"

Rereading what he'd written, he chuckled. "This is

great. It'll add a little humor to my new scrollbook. Readers will love that."

As Athena reached the section of the game board map where her hero statue stood, Homer noticed Poseidon. "You're just the guy I wanted to see!" he told the turquoise-eyed godboy. "Could I ask you a few questions regarding your part in Odysseus's recent troubles? I heard that you stirred up the seas off the island of the Cicones to slow him down the other day."

Poseidon's expression turned to one of delight. There were few things he liked more than attention and praise. "Sure!"

While he and Homer were talking, Athena went to her desk and unfurled her Hero-ology textscroll till she got to the map section. About ten minutes later Homer came to sit across the aisle from her. "What are you doing now?" he asked.

It was hard to think with this author dogging her every move. But since he actually sounded interested and because she wanted his new book, *The Odyssey*, to be as accurate as possible, Athena told him: "Researching."

"Oh," he said, sounding a little bored.

She expanded on her answer. "I'm looking up information on the fastest, safest route to get my hero home to Ithaca."

As Athena spoke, she could hear winds whipping up over on the game board. Good. Those helpful winds would keep Odysseus on course, she thought. And since the crosswinds were all trapped in the bag he'd received, he wouldn't encounter any storms with the potential to be a problem for his ships.

Bringing her attention back to Homer, she said, "There are dangerous currents, sea monsters, and coasts with hazardous rocks that Odysseus will need to avoid.

I don't want him to make any more mistakes if I can help it." She paused. "I guess authors like you have to do research when you write a book too, huh? So you can get the details correct, I mean." She hoped he'd take the hint and be more careful of his facts from now on.

"Details, schmeetails," he said, flicking a careless hand. "I think scrollbook readers care more about excitement, adventure, and funny stuff than accuracy."

Athena glared at him. This was her chance to ask him why he'd left her horse out of his first book. Had he considered it an unimportant detail? It seemed like a pretty exciting event to her! "But if you're telling a nonfiction story about something that really happened, don't you—"

Just then Medusa came over. She stared at Homer through the lenses of her stoneglasses. "You're in my desk," she said, interrupting what Athena had been about to say.

Homer's eyes went to Medusa's snakes, which were standing up on the top of her head, hissing in his direction. "Oh, sorry!" He leaped from her chair.

Medusa sat down in his place. Seeing that Mr. Cyclops wasn't looking, she opened her nail polish and started painting her fingernails green. "You'd better check on your hero," she commented to Athena after a minute, without looking up. It was almost the same thing she'd said last Friday when Odysseus had been in trouble.

"Huh? Why?" Athena's head whipped toward the game board. A crowd that included Aphrodite and Poseidon had gathered around it near the spot where she'd left her hero statue.

"Apparently, Odysseus's men thought there might be gold in that leather bag you gave him, so they opened it when he wasn't looking," said Medusa, casually blowing on her nails to dry them. "The winds inside flew out and

160

caused a storm that drove Odysseus's ships to the land of the Laestrygonians."

"Awesome!" said Homer. He hadn't left after Medusa took back her seat, but had just dragged over an empty chair that belonged to some other student.

"No!" wailed Athena. The Laestrygonians were grumpy giants! She grabbed her Hero-ology scroll, jumped from her desk, and ran to the game board. Homer was right on her heels, still jotting down Medusa's words on the scroll he held.

The giants were already tossing rocks from seaside cliffs toward Odysseus's ships, which had sailed near their island and now floated below the cliffs like sitting ducks. By the time Athena reached the board, eleven of Odysseus's twelve ships had sunk. Only her hero's ship had survived. By now it had sailed to another island.

Athena found a list of islands in her Hero-ology

textscroll and ran a finger down it, trying to determine who resided on the one he'd landed on. "A sorceress named Circe!" she declared after a minute.

Aphrodite leaned over to read the brief description about Circe. "Likes to turn men into swine. Uh-oh."

Sure enough, there were already little pigs running around the island. The sorceress had wasted no time in turning all the men on Odysseus's ship into snuffling, grunting pigs.

"Does anyone see Odysseus? Is he a pig now too?" Athena asked anxiously.

"So was he a pig?" Artemis asked her a few hours later at lunch when Athena was relating the latest awful news about Odysseus.

Athena, Artemis, and Aphrodite were at their usual table, but they were minus Persephone, who had finished lunch earlier and gone to the greenhouse outside in MOA's courtyard to tend to some plants. She was growing them to make garlands to decorate a ring of tall support columns that surrounded the carousel in the Immortal Marketplace. She and Artemis usually had Hero-ology in the morning, but Zeus had taken their classes to the IM to work on the carousel today.

"No, he escaped," Aphrodite explained, since Athena had just taken a bite of a nectarghetti and her mouth was full. "And luckily, he was able to convince Circe to change his crew back to men again too."

"Well, that's a relief," said Artemis.

"Yeah, but Homer took it all down for his new book," said Athena after she swallowed. "It's so embarrassing and truly horrible. In a single class period my hero lost eleven ships and almost all of his men!"

A few minutes later Apollo came over from the

godboy table. After pulling a chair up to the end of the girls' table, he sat on it backward, as if straddling a horse.

"So, who here takes advanced Spell-ology?" he asked, looking around the group.

Athena raised her hand a little, saying, "Me. Fifth period."

"Oh yeah! I remember you did an un-statue curse on Pandora earlier in the year when Medusa turned her to stone, right?" he said. "So maybe you can help me. I want to reverse a difficult curse, but I don't know how to do it."

Athena nodded. "I'll be glad to help, but I'll need more information." She held out a hand and counted three steps on her fingers. "First, who spoke the curse? Second, when was it spoken? And third, what were the exact words of the curse?"

"Me, seven years ago, and I don't remember," said

Apollo. He must've read the concern on Athena's face, because he quickly added, "Yeah, I know. The fact that I don't recall the words of the curse is going to make reversing it hard."

"Try 'impossible,'" Artemis murmured doubtfully.

"Can you at least tell me who or what you cursed?" asked Athena.

"Cassandra," he admitted.

"From the Oracle-O Bakery?" Aphrodite asked in surprise.

Apollo nodded.

"I didn't know you knew her seven years ago," said Artemis.

"I didn't. I mean, I don't remember it, but she says we met in a temple and I cursed her so that no one will believe her fortunes."

Artemis arched an eyebrow. "Or maybe that's just a

story she made up. Pheme told me that no one on Earth believes her fortunes. They all say she's a liar."

"Thing is, I actually think her prophecies *do* come true," said Apollo. "But as far as I can tell, I'm the only one who believes that."

Artemis studied her brother's face a few seconds, and then gasped with sudden realization. "You're in *like* with her, aren't you? You're crushing on a mortal who everyone says is a liar!"

Apollo's cheeks flushed and he stood up. Pointedly ignoring his sister, he said to Athena, "Maybe we could talk in private?"

He and Artemis usually got along great, but he could get huffy when she tried to question his decisions or tell him what to do, Athena knew. But in her opinion Artemis was right to worry. His previous crushes had pretty much ended in disaster!

"You don't have to leave," Artemis mumbled apologetically. "I'll zip my lip."

Apollo slowly sat back down and then flashed Artemis a conciliatory smile. "Okay. Thanks, Sis." Except for occasional squabbles, he and Artemis were really very close.

"I've done a spell-reverse before," Athena mused aloud. "But I've never tried to reverse one that's so old."

"Yeah, you have to be careful about that," Aphrodite added as they all stood and gathered their lunch stuff. "Remember those pleated chitons that were popular when we were all eight years old?" When Athena and Artemis nodded, she went on. "Well, back then this mortal girl asked me to make her fashionable. So I cast a spell to help her and she started wearing pleated chitons. A year later, when the chitons went out of style, she begged me to reverse the spell, but I couldn't."

"So she's still wearing pleated chitons?" Artemis guessed.

Aphrodite nodded. "Worse. And ugly hats, too, thanks to my botched attempt to reverse the spell. So be careful."

Athena and the others couldn't help laughing. To that poor mortal girl, however, it was probably no laughing matter!

"I have an idea where we might get some help," Athena told Apollo. "Come with me." After taking her tray to the tray return and saying bye to Artemis and Aphrodite, Athena went with Apollo to the Spell-ology classroom.

"Ms. Hecate?" Athena asked, popping her head in the door.

Ms. Hecate, the Spell-ology teacher, looked up from the work she was doing at her desk. Her long, wavy black hair was sticking out from her head, gently swirling all around her, like it was floating on water. Only there was no water, of course. Her hair was floating on air! Several pens and scrolls hovered a few inches off her desk, moving around under their own power too.

When she waved Athena and Apollo to come in, though, her hair lowered itself until it hung normally in long waves around her. And the pens and scrolls settled to rest on the desk.

"Just experimenting with a new antigravity spell," she told them. "Can I help you?" The classroom was empty except for the three of them.

After pulling two chairs up to the teacher's desk, Athena and Apollo sat. Then they briefly explained Apollo's problem. Or Cassandra's problem, actually.

"And you say she's a fortune-teller?" Ms. Hecate asked when they had finished. They nodded.

"That's quite a conundrum," she told them. "Old

spells are tricky. Time can warp them. If you knew the words to the spell, it wouldn't be a problem, but—"

They waited quietly as she thought for a minute. The only sound in the room was the drumming of her long, sparkly purple fingernails on the desktop as she concentrated really hard on finding a solution.

Eventually she spoke in a musing voice, "Hmm, a forgotten-curse reverse. Yes, that could work."

"How could what work exactly?" Apollo asked, leaning forward in his chair.

Ms. Hecate's eyes twinkled. "You must get the accursed subject to speak seven prophecies within seven minutes— one for each year that has passed since you spoke your curse. Afterward, say these words to her: 'Esrever esruc nettogrof.'"

Athena ran the words through her mind. "That's 'forgotten-curse reverse,' spoken backward!" she said.

Ms. Hecate nodded. "Oh, and one more thing. The seven-fortune forgotten-curse reverse must take place within a prophecy contest."

Athena looked at Apollo. "Do you think you can get her—um, the *subject*—to take part in a contest. And speak seven prophecies in seven minutes?"

"Worth a try," said Apollo.

"There's no guarantee it will work, but do let me know what happens," Ms. Hecate said. "And good luck!"

After they replaced their chairs at the desks they'd taken them from, Athena and Apollo thanked the teacher. Then they hurried outside to the courtyard. The students who were assigned to work on the carousel were starting to leave for the Immortal Marketplace. Athena spotted Aphrodite and Persephone sitting side by side on a stone bench, putting on pairs of winged sandals. Long, leafy garlands with colorful flowers lay in a heap beside them.

Artemis was calling her milk-white, golden-horned deer to her chariot. Quickly Apollo jumped into the back of it along with Hades, Poseidon, and Ares.

Homer climbed inside too. "Can I drive?" he asked Artemis as she hitched her deer to pull them.

Everyone within hearing, including Athena, gasped. Artemis never let anyone drive her chariot! Especially not after a stowaway who'd come to MOA in the back of Hermes' delivery chariot had "borrowed" her chariot and almost wrecked it.

"Absolutely not," Artemis told him firmly. She glanced at Athena. "Want to ride with us?"

"No, that's okay," said Athena, taking a few steps backward. "Looks pretty crowded in there already. I'll wing it with Aphrodite and Persephone instead."

Artemis sent her a knowing grin, probably guessing that she wanted a break from Homer's company.

"Okay! See you there!" With that, she whistled to her team of deer and they whisked the chariot off toward the Immortal Marketplace.

Athena called to Persephone and Aphrodite to wait up, then ran back up MOA's front granite steps. Pushing through the heavy bronze front doors, she shucked off her sandals, and then grabbed winged sandals from a big basket of them over by the wall. As soon as she slipped them on, the sandals' straps twined around her ankles, and silver wings at her heels began to flap. With her feet hovering several inches above the ground, she zipped back out to the courtyard to join her two friends.

She, Aphrodite, and Persephone gathered the garlands Persephone had made in their arms, rose higher, and sped off down Mount Olympus. The ends of the long flowery garlands streamed out behind them as they flew across the sky toward the Immortal Marketplace.

8

The Prophecy Contest

Cassandra

*B*AM! *BAM!* SOMEONE WAS HAMMERING. IT WAS

Tuesday afternoon, and the students from Mount Olympus Academy were back at the IM, working on their carousel. Cassandra could see them through the store window of the scrollbook shop as she half-listened to more of Homer's many demands for this Saturday's signing.

"I want a big platter of Oracle-O cookies set here and a

jar of jelly beans here," Homer was saying now. He drew her attention to spots on either end of the big decorative table that she and Helenus had set up for the book signing. "So things are balanced. Symmetrical."

"Sure," Cassandra said distractedly. When she glanced out the window again, Persephone was hanging long festive swags of flowers and greenery on columns around the carousel in the atrium area. And Hades was using a hammer to nail the greenery in place.

Other students were waving their arms around and chanting spells to magically paint or decorate their animals or the carousel itself. Yesterday afternoon Zeus had been testing the carousel mechanics and had made the platform with the animals turn a few times. Luckily, Athena's offensive horse had wound up on the opposite side of the carousel, so Cassandra couldn't see it right now.

"Make sure the cookie icing and all the jelly beans

are blue," Homer said, interrupting her thoughts. "To go with my hair, which matches the blue ribbon tie on my *Iliad* scrollbooks."

Cassandra glanced from the window to his spiky blue hair, and then to the ribbon tie on the single copy of his scrollbook lying on the table next to Mr. Euripedes' hourglass. He'd bought it at Magical Wagical, and it had a cool timer bell. She frowned. "The cookie icing won't be a problem. But Sweetza Treatza is the candy store here in the IM, and they only sell multicolored jelly beans, all mixed together. So—"

But Homer wasn't listening. "This chair won't do," he announced as he tried out the big oak chair behind the table.

"What's wrong with it?"

He frowned, squirming around on its seat. "For one thing it's not blue like I wanted. Don't you have a chair that looks more author-ish? A blue one with a gold tasseled cushion, maybe?"

Grrr. How was he expecting her to come up with the exact chair he wanted? Did he think she could magic one up like those immortals out in the atrium could have?

The book event wasn't for four more days. She wasn't sure she'd survive till then with this picky pompous pipsqueak author driving her crazy. However, earlier this morning her mom had gone to speak with Zeus at MOA about some details of the event. So it was up to Cassandra to humor Homer as much as she could. After all, her mom had entrusted her with the job of being his assistant. Which pretty much meant catering to his every whim.

Homer sighed. "And here in the center of the table where I can smell them, I'd like three scented candles. The calming aromatherapy kind."

The calming aromatherapy kind? All of a sudden

Cassandra realized something. Homer was nervous. Saturday was going to be a big day for him as well as for her family's store. Naturally he just wanted everything to go right. So did her mom. So did Cassandra.

"German chamomile candles are blue, so I'll try to get some of those," she said helpfully. "And maybe I can borrow a blue chair with a gold cushion from the Chairs & Thrones Galore Store in the IM. I'll ask," she added.

Homer nodded gratefully, then picked up a blue quill pen and the partly blank notescroll he always seemed to keep handy. He began practicing ways to write his auto-graph. He showed her three different signature samples, one in big blocky letters, one swirly, and a scribbled one that was completely unreadable except for the *H* at the beginning.

"Which autograph style do you think I should use on Saturday during my signing?" he asked.

"Does it really matter?"

"Yes! Every detail counts. This book has to do well, or my editor won't publish my next one." He hesitated, then leaned toward her earnestly. "You claim you can see the future, right? So tell me which signature will bring me the most success."

"Um, sure," said Cassandra. She really hadn't realized how much pressure he was under! "Maybe the swirly one?" she said.

"Liar, liar, chiton on fire," said a voice. She looked over to see that one of her least favorite people was back. That annoying Agamemnon. He grinned at her, then said to Homer, "If I were you, I wouldn't trust her. She's always wrong. And she's bad luck, too. She told me so herself."

Homer considered the signatures again, looking unsure now.

Laodice had hinted that Agamemnon liked Cassandra.

However, if this was his idea of flirting, he was totally bad at it! Didn't he know he was hurting her feelings? This was *not* a good way to get a girl's attention!

"Leave her alone," said Helenus, coming in behind Agamemnon.

And suddenly Apollo appeared too. "There you are," he called to Cassandra as he leaned through the new arched opening that led from the bakery into the bookshop. His eyes left hers to scan the other faces in the room, as if he sensed a problem in the making. Then he sniffed the air. "I smell cinnamon," he said.

Cassandra sniffed the air too, then cocked her head uncertainly. "Maybe it's the cookies over in the bakery?"

Artemis's head popped up behind her brother's. "No, it means he's going to predict something," she said.

Really? That was interesting! thought Cassandra. Until that moment she hadn't realized that Apollo's predictions were preceded by a scent too!

Squeezing his eyes shut, Apollo fell silent. Then, in a dramatic tone, he called out, "I predict that Cassandra and I are about to engage in a prophecy contest. Actually, that's not a real prediction. What I meant to say was that I *challenge* her to a contest. We'll take turns to see who can give the most predictions within seven minutes!"

"Awesome!" said Homer, perking up. He picked up his pen again, poised to write everything they did or said as it happened. And behind Apollo, Pheme appeared.

"She can't," said Helenus. "She's not allowed."

"Oh, really?" said Apollo. He looked ready to argue.

"He's right," said Cassandra. "My mom says—"

"Why don't all *three* of you have a contest?" Agamemnon butted in. Trying to stir up more trouble, no doubt. He glanced from Helenus to Cassandra to Apollo.

Cassandra was already shaking her head when she

smelled peppermints. A vision came to her in a flash. Homer must've guessed what was going on in her head because he immediately upended Mr. Euripedes' hourglass, setting its timer for seven minutes.

"The sorceress Circe has sent the hero Odysseus to the Underworld!" Cassandra blurted.

Every eye turned her way. She put her hand over her mouth, startled at the words she'd spoken. Just then, Pheme dashed out into the IM, no doubt to tell everyone what was happening in there.

Homer grinned from ear to ear. "Excellent! The contest has begun! Who'll go second? Let's see who can best predict what will happen to Athena's hero on his way home to Ithaca."

"You're on!" said Helenus, apparently deciding to join in.

"Me too. But only if Cassandra stays in," Apollo insisted.

Helenus looked torn. *Why?* Cassandra wondered.

Was he afraid he would lose to her as well as to Apollo? No one could expect to win in a contest if they were competing against the godboy of prophecy, but losing to her would be a blow to Helenus's ego. Still, it would boost his reputation as a fortune-teller to simply *be* in a contest with Apollo!

The scrollbook store began to fill with mortals and immortals alike as Pheme spread the news about Apollo's prophecy contest challenge.

"But I—" Cassandra began. For her this contest was likely to only bring trouble. Her mom would be mad at her for breaking her promise *not* to prophesy. And in the end, everyone would think she was lying, no matter what truths she spoke. Still, she longed for the chance to speak her prophecies aloud for a change.

Scanning the crowd, she glimpsed Athena and Artemis with their heads together, whispering. She caught a couple of their words: "Odysseus . . . Underworld." Artemis had to be filling Athena in on the first prophecy Cassandra had spoken. She saw Andromache in the crowd behind them, eavesdropping.

Apollo's voice rang out, drawing everyone's attention. "For my first prophecy I predict that if Cassandra tells six more prophecies before the end of our contest, it will bring the Oracle-O Bakery and Scrollbooks seven years of good luck!"

Cassandra's eyes went wide. Seven years of good luck was a lot. With that at stake she absolutely had to give this contest a try, regardless of how others (particularly her mom) might feel about her participation!

When the scent of peppermints wafted to her again, she heard herself say, "After leaving the Underworld, Odysseus will sail to the land of the Sirens."

"What?" Athena exclaimed in a horrified voice. Many

in the audience gasped, thinking Odysseus was doomed. The Sirens were women whose songs enchanted passing sailors into steering their ships directly into giant rocks along the coastline, where they'd crash and sink.

"All the sailors on his ship will stuff beeswax into their ears, so they won't hear the song," said Apollo.

"Wait! It was my turn," said Helenus.

"Do two to catch up," Cassandra suggested. Her eyes flicked to the hourglass. Four and a half minutes left. "And hurry."

Helenus nodded, and then a second later he said, "The Sirens will be beautiful. And their songs will be too."

More of his vague fortunes, thought Cassandra. And they were really descriptions more than predictions. Agamemnon's eyebrows rose, and he shot Helenus a skeptical look that suggested even he thought what Helenus had said was pretty lame.

To Cassandra's surprise she felt a flash of irritation toward Agamemnon on her brother's behalf. So what if Helenus wasn't really very good at this? It was the best he could do! It was okay for her to criticize him. She was his *sister*, so it went with the territory. But even though she considered some of her brother's prophecies kind of dumb too, she didn't want anyone else to criticize him. She sent her brother an encouraging smile.

Then she smelled peppermints again. "Uh-oh!" she said as a new vision flashed before her eyes.

"What is it?" Athena demanded. She was looking really worried for her hero by now.

"Odysseus will refuse to use the beeswax so he can hear the Siren's glorious songs," Cassandra explained gently. Although she was still ticked at Athena over the Trojan horse, she didn't enjoy giving anyone bad news. Besides, her prophecies weren't *causing* these things to happen to Odysseus. These events she foretold would come true whether predicted or not!

"He will tie himself to the mast instead," said Apollo. "In hopes that being bound will stop him from steering the boat into the rocks!"

"The moon and stars will shine brightly above him," Helenus put in.

"That fool!" an older man in the crowd whispered. Cassandra wasn't sure if he was referring to Odysseus, or to Helenus because of his useless "prediction."

Athena's face had gone pale. "Oh, no!" she wailed before she dashed from the shop. There was no way she would make it back to MOA in time to advise her hero, Cassandra knew. These things were going to happen right away. Within minutes, in fact.

Her gaze met Andromache's. She looked as uncertain as Cassandra felt. Both girls had been kind of annoyed at Athena. But now, like Cassandra, maybe Andromache was feeling bad for the goddessgirl.

The peppermint smell came again. "Odysseus will make it safely past the Sirens," Cassandra prophesied. "Then his ship will pass between a six-headed sea monster named Scylla and a giant whirlpool named Charybdis."

She kind of wished Athena had waited long enough to hear that Odysseus would be safe from the Sirens. Not that Athena would have believed Cassandra. Not for long, anyway. She gazed at the faces around her. Did anyone here believe her? Caught up in the moment, they seemed to have forgotten that they thought her a liar. They'd likely remember soon, she thought glumly. And the fortunes she'd spoken would get all twisted around in their heads.

"Odysseus will avoid the whirlpool, knowing it could drown his ship. But Scylla will devour six of his sailors," Apollo announced.

There was a small silence as everyone digested this horrific prophecy. How awful! Maybe it was better that Athena hadn't stayed after all, thought Cassandra.

"His ship will stop at the island where Helios the sun god lives," said Helenus. "While Odysseus takes a nap, his men will steal some of Helios's prize cattle."

Apollo gave him a high five. "Good one."

It *was* a pretty good prophecy, Cassandra thought. Especially for her brother. She flashed him a smile.

Then suddenly the peppermint smell came again and she foresaw more trouble. "Helios will become so angry that he'll threaten to never again let his sun chariot rise in the sky. As a punishment Zeus will hurl a bolt of lightning at Odysseus's ship."

More gasps sounded.

Quickly Apollo took his turn. "The ship will sink."

"Odysseus will have to fight for his life," said Helenus.

Everyone groaned. Would Odysseus suffer through all these ordeals just to die in the end? Was he doomed never to make it home? All eyes swung in Cassandra's direction, waiting to hear what she'd say now.

The smell of peppermints was stronger than ever as Cassandra began her sixth prophecy. "Odysseus will swim safely to the island of Ogygia and meet a possessive nymph named Calypso. She will try to make him immortal and keep him there forever!"

Apollo took a deep breath. Was the smell of cinnamon as strong for him as peppermint was for her whenever a prophecy filled her mind? Cassandra wondered.

"Odysseus will escape," Apollo assured everyone who'd gathered in the store. "But Poseidon will stir up a terrible storm with his trident, and Odysseus will be forced to swim ashore."

The immortals in the crowd murmured at this, some

sounding pleased at what the god of the sea would do, and others sounding upset. It depended on who they were rooting for—Athena or Poseidon. From what she overheard, Cassandra guessed there was some kind of rivalry going on between those two immortals in their Hero-ology class that had to do with Odysseus's travels.

"The waves will be high, the current strong from the storm," added Helenus. It was another one of his more descriptive than predictive prophecies.

Cassandra could feel the tense excitement in the room as she spoke her seventh fortune. The one that Apollo had predicted would ensure good luck for her family for seven years! "When Odysseus gets home, he will discover that everyone believes him to be dead, and that dozens of his enemies have been vying to marry his wife, Penelope, so that they can claim his riches!"

Diiing! Cassandra glanced at the hourglass as its

magic timer bell rang. She'd made it. Seven prophecies in seven minutes!

Excited murmurs filled the crowd. "How dare they! That's not right!" someone said. Then all faces whipped Apollo's way. Everyone was dying to hear his next prediction. But Apollo was silent.

"What happens next?" a mortal woman asked anxiously.

Apollo shook his head. "I can see no more."

Cassandra waited for another whiff of peppermints, but it didn't come. "I can see no further into the future either," she said.

"Me neither," Helenus admitted.

"Cassandra has the last prediction, then. She wins!" Apollo declared, throwing his arms wide.

Homer had been busy during the whole contest scribbling notes on his scroll, Cassandra realized now. How awesome that she'd helped him tell some of Odysseus's adventures!

"Esrever esruc nettogrof," said Apollo.

Huh? Cassandra looked around to see that he had come over to stand beside her. "What did you say?" she asked him.

Before he could reply, they heard shrieks. Wild magical winds came swirling through the Immortal Marketplace, whipping through the atrium and around the carousel, teasing hair, and lifting the hems of chitons and tunics alike. The winds rattled outside the scrollbook shop door until someone opened it and let them in.

We bring reports

From MOA

Of a hero's

Troubles far away.

The winds then proceeded to tell the exact same facts that all three contestants in the contest had spoken. Now that Cassandra's predictions were confirmed, everyone would have to believe she was telling the truth, she hoped. Right?

Wrong. Only minutes had passed since her last prediction. But even so there were rumblings of doubt from the crowd. Despite the news brought by the magic winds, which echoed what all three of the contestants had stated in their prophecies, people were already starting to mis-remember the things Cassandra had said. Some complained that they'd actually been lies!

"She said that Circe sent Odysseus up to the heavens, right? But really he went to the Underworld."

"Yeah, and then she claimed that his enemies wanted to give away all of Odysseus's riches."

"She's got to be wrong," someone grumbled. "They'd

keep his riches if they got their hands on them!"

Argh! As usual, her fortunes were being misinterpreted!

Cassandra glanced at Apollo and saw that he looked even more upset than she felt. "I'm sorry," he told her. "I guess my plan didn't work."

She shrugged. "Seven years of good luck would've been great, but . . . well . . . easy come, easy go." She was surprised at how well she was taking this. But she'd had pretty low expectations for the outcome of the contest anyway.

"No, you don't understand," said Apollo. He ran his fingers through his hair, looking frustrated. "The Spell-ology teacher at MOA said that if I got you to say seven prophecies during a contest, and then I said 'Esrever esruc nettogrof,' which is 'forgotten-curse reverse' backward, it might reverse the curse I put on you."

"Oh." Now she really *was* disappointed! But how nice that he'd gone to that trouble to try to help her. "So you've finally remembered putting the curse on me?"

He shook his head. "If only I did. It would make the curse reversible. One good thing, though, is that your family will still have seven years of good luck. I can make that part come true."

She brightened some. "Well, that's good. Thanks." Deep inside, though, it hurt to know that her prophecies were still doomed to not be believed and would forever go unheeded. She was tired of being the bearer of bad news as well as being thought a liar. Maybe she should just give up on making prophecies!

9

Going Wild!

Cassandra

FINALLY! IT WAS SATURDAY, THE DAY OF THE BIG author event at Oracle-O Bakery and Scrollbooks. The carousel was complete. Having just run a last-minute errand for her mom in the IM, Cassandra took time to circle around the carousel, admiring it.

Scenic paintings atop the carousel's peaked roof depicted the glorious exploits of the gods. She could see Zeus bringing down a Titan with one of his mighty thunderbolts, and Helios driving his sun chariot across the sky. And there was Athena dressed for battle, wearing a pointy helmet and holding a shield. She also clutched a spear, while on her shoulder there perched an owl. The scenes inspired awe, which was probably what they were *meant* to do!

Colorful flowers, rainbows, and cute kittens had been carved around the roof's edge. She'd seen Persephone and Iris creating those all week. And the leafy garlands Persephone and Hades had wound around nearby columns in the atrium looked so festive and pretty!

But the animal rides were Cassandra's favorite part. All were bigger than she was and had been painted and polished till they gleamed. Stately standers, which were the rides that didn't go up and down on their poles, stood on the platform closest to the carousel's center.

Jumpers—the rides that could pump up and down on their poles—stood along the outer edge. She stopped beside Athena's horse, and her lips twisted.

"Hi," said Athena, surprising her.

Cassandra had been so busy looking around at the animals that she hadn't seen Athena sitting on the edge of the platform. She must've only just arrived at the IM because she was tying back the wings of her sandals so they would stop flapping, thus keeping her on the ground.

When Athena finally stood, she gestured to her horse. "So, what do you think?"

"I hate it." The words tumbled from Cassandra's lips before she could think to temper them. It was one thing to grumble in private about a goddess, but it was quite unwise to speak this way to her face! She rushed to explain. "It reminds me of the war, and I'm afraid it will make everyone remember my Trojan horse prediction."

Would Athena smite her now for her audacity? Luckily, she wasn't dressed for battle like in the carousel painting.

To Cassandra's surprise Athena didn't get mad at all. Instead her blue-gray eyes softened. "Oh, I'm so sorry," she said. "I didn't mean . . . I never thought of that. I suppose we immortals get so involved with ourselves that we sometimes forget the feelings of mortals down here on Earth. I should know better, because until my dad summoned me to MOA earlier this year, I'd always thought I was mortal myself! So do you want me to take it off the carousel?"

"You'd take off the horse?" Cassandra asked, taken aback. "For me?"

Athena nodded. "I don't want to cause you trouble."

Hearing this kind offer, Cassandra finally realized she'd really, truly misjudged Athena.

The goddessgirl surveyed the carousel. "Hmm.

Removing it will leave a big gap between animals on the carousel, though. My dad won't be pleased."

They both looked over at the red-and-white-striped ticket booth about ten feet away. Zeus was manning it, and he appeared to be having a blast with the little mortal and immortal kids who'd gathered around in anticipation of the carousel rides.

When he gave the signal, a whole bunch of them dashed over to drop their tickets into the ticket box at the front of the line. Then they rushed onto the carousel, quickly claiming the animals they most wanted to ride. The MOA students who'd been working on the carousel all week had been standing around the fringes of it, talking to visitors about the project, but now they moved closer to help the children onto the animals.

Apollo tossed a giggling little mortal girl onto the back of his raven. Dionysus chatted with a boy who'd hopped onto his leopard's back. Artemis handed the reins to an elderly woman who'd come to sit in her deer-and-chariot ride. All the MOA students seemed eager to help young and old alike take pleasure in what they'd made.

How nice, thought Cassandra. And how cool that the immortals had decided that the carousel would remain in the marketplace forever for all to enjoy!

Just then an excited little mortal boy came up to Athena. "I've been waiting and waiting to ride your horse," he said in a rush. After sticking his foot into the stirrup, he flung himself onto its saddle. Then he waved to someone in the crowd. "Look at me, Mommy!"

"I'm next on the horse!" called another boy from the sidelines.

"Then me!" called a girl.

Athena sent Cassandra a questioning look, silently asking if she wanted her to tell the kids they couldn't have their ride. She appeared ready to remove the horse if that's what Cassandra wanted.

So what *did* she want?

Suddenly the carousel started moving, making the decision for her. Zeus had flipped the switch in the ticket booth to turn it on. Athena hopped off the platform just in time as the carousel began to whirl around in a flash of mirrors, jewels, and colors. Shouts of delight rose up from every rider.

Cassandra's lips curved, and she shook her head. "They're having too much fun. I couldn't ruin that. It's enough to know you were willing to remove the horse for the sake of my feelings. That you didn't create it just to—"

"Hurt you? I didn't," Athena said earnestly. "Honest."

Cassandra smiled even wider at her, feeling somehow lighter and freer as her long-held resentment against this girl slid away for good. "I believe you."

A few seconds later Homer called to Cassandra from the main door of the scrollbook shop. His publicist was roaming the atrium, trying to beckon shoppers inside to buy copies of *The Iliad*. So far no one was really paying attention to him. With a wave Cassandra dashed off. "Duty calls," she shouted back to Athena, who grinned and waved in return.

"Where are the cookies?" Homer demanded the moment Cassandra reached him.

"I'll get them," she promised as they stepped inside. A peek around the scrollbook store showed a large, neat stack of scrollbooks tied with blue ribbons on the long table—the published copies of his *Iliad*. But no one was yet in line to buy one. And Homer looked super-nervous about that fact.

She dashed through the archway opening and over to the cookie counter in the bakery, where she grabbed the big basket of blue fortune cookies Andromache had made for the event. Laodice and Helenus were so busy doing brisk cookie sales that they didn't even notice her. Their mom was fielding reporters from *Greekly Weekly News* and *Teen Scrollazine,* a big smile on her face. "Be sure to get the store sign in your sketches," she called out to the artists covering the event. She was so great at promoting the store!

Why . . . her mom was totally happy here! Cassandra realized. So were Laodice and Helenus. None of them wanted to return to war-torn Troy. Did she still want to? For the first time she wasn't sure.

"I haven't sold a single copy," Homer whispered to her a minute later as they both sat at the table piled high with *Iliad* scrollbooks.

He looked really rattled. Was he concerned that he wouldn't sell any? "Don't worry," Cassandra told him kindly. "I predict that your book signing will be a success."

However, she was disturbed at the peppermint-scented prophecy that actually came into her mind. *A sheep with cosmetics on its face will run wild?* Maybe this image had only sprung into her head because of Odysseus's sheep-riding adventure on the island with the Cyclops, which everyone was still talking about. She ignored it as best she could.

"Here come some people," she told Homer as a group entered the scrollbook shop and approached the table.

He smiled hopefully at them.

"Excuse me. Where's the bathroom?" the first man asked.

Homer's face fell.

As Cassandra directed the man to the nearest bathroom, a woman walked over to Homer, gazing at the scrollbooks. "Hi. Are you an author?" she asked.

"Yes!" said Homer, brightening.

"Did you write that play *Electra*? It was sooo good!"

"No, that's by Euripides. I wrote *The Iliad*."

The woman frowned. *"The Silly Ad?"* Her face lit up again. "Haven't heard of it. But I love silly scrollbooks almost as much as tragedies. I'll take two copies."

After the woman left, Cassandra and Homer looked at each other.

"Cha-ching! My first sale!" said Homer, punching his fist in the air. "I'm a real author!"

And suddenly dozens of people were lining up to buy a copy of *The Iliad*, just as she'd foreseen would happen, over a week ago.

Most of the customers gushed over the excerpts they'd read of the scrollbook in *Teen Scrollazine* or the *Greekly Weekly News*, which thrilled Homer to no end. He sat up straighter in his chair and seemed to slowly regain his usual cocky confidence. Odysseus was a hot topic, and many of those waiting for autographs were clamoring for news of the sequel as rumors about Athena's hero's exciting adventures circulated. Everyone who came up to get a signed copy of the scrollbook wanted to know how Odysseus's final homecoming in Ithaca would turn out.

"You'll have to read *The Odyssey* after it's published," Homer would say mysteriously. Then Cassandra would take their payment and give them one of the blue Oracle-O cookies.

Every time someone opened a cookie, it said, "You are going to love *The Iliad*." There were prizes in some of the cookies too, with a few people winning free scrollbooks from the shop.

One hour later the bookstore's copies of *The Iliad* were sold out! A thrilled-looking Homer was ushered off by his publicist to be interviewed a final time by the reporters.

Cassandra breathed a big sigh of relief and sat back in her chair, feeling happy with the way the signing had gone.

"The ultimate embarrassment payback is underway," a voice whispered from behind her.

Startled, she turned to see Andromache peeking out from one of the scrollbook shelves.

Cassandra leaped up and pulled Andromache aside. "About that," she told her friend. "Now that I've gotten to know a few of these immortals, I just don't feel the same way I used to about them. They were easy to dislike when we didn't know them, but now—"

"So, what are you saying?" Andromache interrupted.

Taking a deep breath, Cassandra said, "That I've decided to forget about payback. I'm tired of being mad. Because it only makes me, well, madder."

Andromache's eyes went wide. "I wish I'd known that earlier. I only did what I did for you!" she blurted.

"For me? What did you do?" Cassandra asked, feeling confused.

"Not *just* for you, I guess," Andromache admitted. "For me, too."

"C'mon, spill. What did you do?" Cassandra demanded, her stomach sinking.

"Well, remember those lemon fortunes you wrote on that polka-dot papyrus last Saturday in the bakery? The ones we laughed about?"

Cassandra nodded.

"I sort of did something with them," said Andromache.

"Oh no! You didn't give them to Homer to put on the game board, did you?" Cassandra guessed in horror.

"Um, no. But I—" Andromache began. But before she could go on, they heard strange sounds in the atrium.

Animal sounds, people shrieking in surprise, and really weird laughter.

"Uh-oh," Andromache muttered in a guilty tone.

As they ran out the bookshop door to see what was going on, Athena's carousel horse galloped past, its mane flying. It was laughing! Pan's sheep dashed by and went into Cleo's Cosmetics. Meanwhile, Dionysus's leopard was batting playfully at the ends of the garlands Persephone had hung up.

The carousel rides had come alive. And gone wild! They still looked like fanciful carousel animals, not real ones. Yet they were running amok through the market-place, rambunctiously zooming here and there and get-ting into mischief. Immortals and mortals alike were chasing them down, trying to corral them.

"Why is this happening?" asked Cassandra, shocked.

"It's my fault," whispered Andromache. "I took the

lemon fortunes you wrote and passed them out to the immortals they were meant for a few minutes ago. I thought that embarrassing them would make us both feel better."

Cassandra could only watch in dismay as, one by one, her fortunes came true, starting with Pan's sheep. It ran out of Cleo's Cosmetics with lip gloss around its mouth. Aphrodite was hot on its trail.

"It nibbled all of Cleo's lip glosses to stubs!" Aphrodite informed the crowd. "Seemed to like the green ones best. Maybe they looked like grass?" She had gotten smeared with lip gloss herself while trying to chase the sheep. She looked like she was wearing clown makeup!

"'Aphrodite will be embarrassed by really *baaad* makeup,'" Cassandra murmured to herself. That was one of the fortunes she'd written last Saturday!

"We have to help capture the animals!" she said

firmly. Andromache nodded and the two girls dashed off to help.

Crash! Before they could accomplish anything, Athena's horse ran smack into a wall and splintered into a dozen pieces.

Cassandra groaned, recalling what she'd written. *Athena's horse will crack itself up.* And then she saw Apollo standing there, looking shocked. He was moving his lips, but no words were coming out. *"'Apollo will stand speechless in the middle of chaos.'"* she murmured.

"I'm so sorry!" moaned Andromache, overhearing.

Cassandra gave her hand a squeeze. "It's my fault too. I shouldn't have written those lemon predictions." Of course, if Andromache hadn't given them to the immortals, they wouldn't have come true. So they shared the blame for what had happened.

Eventually the goddessgirls and godboys began

casting spells to corral the carousel animals. One by one the animals voluntarily returned to their perches on the carousel and posed, still again. Soon everything was calm. It was almost as if the rampage had never occurred. Except for the splotches of lip gloss that remained around the sheep's mouth, and the missing spot where Athena's horse used to be. And, of course, the entire Immortal Marketplace was a mess!

Cassandra turned to see her mom, Zeus, and Hera standing beside her. She didn't want to, but she was going to have to take responsibility for this. Even if Andromache *had* been the one to distribute the fortunes, *she'd* been the one to write them. But before she could open her mouth, Zeus spread his muscled arms wide.

"Genius!" he boomed. "This was the best finale to the best event I've ever come up with!" He turned to Hera. "I think you should let me help plan your weddings from now on. They'd be much more exciting, don't you think, sugarplum?"

"They certainly would be," Hera said judiciously.

As it turned out, no one guessed that the mess had anything to do with Cassandra or her predictions. Instead, everyone chalked up the animals going berserk to everything from a publicity stunt by Homer's publicist to Zeus unleashing some magic that had gone a little out of control. Though the reasons varied wildly, people thought the resulting chaos was just part of the overall event. And the reporters had gotten it all down for the news.

Right away, immortals and mortals began working side by side to clean up the Immortal Marketplace. There was much giggling and even gasps of delight as immortals performed amazing feats of magic.

Over by the pile of bits that had been her horse, Athena began to twirl in a slow circle, chanting:

"Pieces join. Horse uncrack.

Then to the carousel, trot on back!"

At her command, the pieces of her carousel horse rose into the air alongside her and whirled like a small tornado, faster and faster. *Snap!* All at once, they reattached themselves perfectly to form her horse exactly as it was before. It trotted obediently to the carousel, taking its place there once again.

In Cleo's Cosmetics, Aphrodite gracefully raised both arms and gestured around the store, saying:

"Lip gloss, powder, eye shadow, too,

Be as you were, all cute and new."

Instantly makeup mirrors un-cracked, and lip gloss stubs reshaped themselves to become new again. Eye shadow and face powder puffed from the counters into the air and then back into their original containers.

Over in Mighty Fighty, Apollo regained his voice and did an unspell:

> *"Shields flatten.*
> *Spears unbend.*
> *Bring this destruction*
> *To an end!"*

Even as his words were dying away, dents smoothed out of shields. Spears that had been bent by wild carousel animals straightened themselves. Suits of armor creaked back into their original shapes.

In no time, all was back to normal and the Marketplace was sparkling clean! As Cassandra looked around the IM at everyone happily chatting together, she realized that this was her home now. And that the people here—both mortal and immortal—were actually pretty nice. Just look how everyone had pitched in to help! She could make friends here if she tried. . . .

Cassandra's eyes lit on Athena, who was heading her way. "Can you come back to MOA with me?" Athena asked when she reached her. "I have to get Odysseus home fast, and I think you could help guide me in that." She must've seen the doubt in Cassandra's eyes because she quickly added, "Apollo has faith in your predictions and that's good enough for me."

Cassandra's heart lifted. The mortals nearby who had overheard caught their breath. It was a great honor to be invited to Mount Olympus Academy. And even sweeter, it was because of her fortune-telling talents!

"Yes! I'd love to come!" she told Athena.

10

Reverse the Curse

Cassandra

THE WIND WHISTLED IN CASSANDRA'S EARS and whipped her fire-gold hair as she, Athena, and Aphrodite winged their way toward Mount Olympus Academy after the author event.

Athena had purchased magic sandals for Cassandra in Magical Wagical before they'd left the IM. Although the sandals normally didn't work for mortals, the wings on Cassandra's sandals began to flap as soon as Athena and Aphrodite stood on either side of her and grasped her hands.

As they whooshed past boulders and trees, Cassandra turned her head this way and that. "This is the most amazing way to travel ever!" she exclaimed, marveling at the sights below and the speed at which they flew.

Hermes' delivery chariot was flying right behind them, carrying Homer, who was bouncing here and there among a bunch of letters and packages also bound for MOA. And all around them were other immortals traveling homeward in the same direction.

Cassandra spotted Apollo, and he waved to her from the back of Artemis's chariot, where he sat with Poseidon, Ares, Hades, and Persephone. Cassandra couldn't wave back since she had to hold the goddess-girls' hands to remain aloft, so she sent him a big smile instead. Artemis noticed and for some reason frowned at her for doing that.

But Cassandra didn't have time to wonder why, because the most awesome sight of all appeared right then, as they neared the end of their trip. It was the majestic Academy itself! Though she'd seen it before when she'd come for Zeus and Hera's wedding, it was a sight that never failed to thrill. It gleamed in the afternoon sunlight atop the highest mountain in Greece. Built of polished white stone, it was five stories tall and surrounded on all sides by dozens of Ionic columns. Low-relief friezes showing dramatic figures of immortals had been chiseled from marble just below the building's peaked rooftop.

She and her two goddessgirl companions went lower and touched down minutes later, skidding to a stop in the courtyard. After loosening the straps at their ankles,

Athena and Aphrodite looped them over the silver wings to hold them in place so the girls could walk at a normal speed. Of course, Cassandra didn't have to do anything. Her wings stopped flapping the moment her two immortal companions released her hands.

"We'll go straight to the Hero-ology classroom, okay?" Athena said. She seemed a little stressed out. But who wouldn't be, with the fate of a hero in their hands! She and Aphrodite led Cassandra up the front granite stairs and into the Academy, then down a long hall.

Cassandra had forgotten just how beautiful MOA was! Shiny marble tile floors. Golden fountains. A domed ceiling covered with paintings depicting the awe-inspiring feats of the gods and goddesses. One scene showed them battling giants that were storming Mount Olympus carrying torches and spears. Another showed Zeus driving a chariot pulled by four white horses across the sky as he hurled thunderbolts into the clouds.

Soon the girls entered a classroom. Homer, Poseidon, Artemis, Apollo, and some of the other immortals who'd come from the IM followed them inside. They all went over to a three-dimensional map that completely covered a big table in the center of the room. As they gathered around to study it, Cassandra realized that this must be the game board she'd heard so much about.

Athena pointed at the statue of Odysseus. He was still wandering around in Ithaca. "My hero hasn't moved much since your last prophecy in the contest," she said, relieved. Then she pointed to a ship in the harbor off the coast. "The friendly sailors on that ship are the ones that gave my hero a ride home. I should thank them by help- ing them in some way."

But as she paused to think of a proper "thank-you," the turquoise-eyed Poseidon aimed the pointy end of his trident at the little ship and muttered some magic. The ship turned into a rock!

"That's for helping Odysseus," Poseidon told the sailors.

Athena and Aphrodite whirled around, their eyes flashing at him. "That was just plain mean!" said Athena.

Poseidon smirked. "The better to help my grade!"

Cassandra watched all this in amazement. So this was how the immortals guided the fortunes of mortals? According to their whims? It all seemed so random. But then that was kind of how life was, she supposed.

Athena turned her back on Poseidon and looked at Cassandra. "Your last fortune in the prophecy contest said that when Odysseus got to Ithaca, he would discover that everyone believed he'd lived through the war."

"And that his enemies were not after his riches or his wife, Penelope," added Aphrodite.

Athena must have read the dismay on Cassandra's face, because she said, "Or did we mis-remember that?"

"Big-time," said Cassandra, nodding. It had been twenty-four hours since they'd heard her predictions, so of course they'd gotten them all wrong by now. "His enemies think he's dead," she explained. "And they're still after his riches and his wife."

"Believe her," Apollo urged. Athena and Aphrodite looked over at him and then back at Cassandra.

"Okay, we'll roll with it," said Athena. "So, any idea what'll happen next?"

Cassandra started to admit that she didn't know, but then suddenly she smelled peppermints. "You will disguise Odysseus as an old beggar so he can check how things stand with his wife and kingdom," she told Athena.

The goddessgirl drew in a sharp breath, apparently caught off guard by Cassandra's near-instant prediction.

"Quick! Do it before we mis-remember what she said," Aphrodite advised.

Athena nodded, and did as Cassandra had predicted.

"Penelope doesn't want to marry anyone. She still loves Odysseus," Cassandra went on as more prophetic information filled her head.

At this she heard Aphrodite sigh happily and say, "I knew it!"

"But the suitors are putting on pressure," Cassandra went on. "So Penelope will declare that whoever can string Odysseus's powerful bow and shoot an arrow through twelve axe handles can marry her and become the new king of Ithaca."

As Cassandra continued to predict events, Homer hastily jotted them down in his notescroll. Meanwhile Athena made moves on the game board to reflect the prophecies.

226

"What next?" Homer asked breathlessly when Cassandra paused for a few seconds.

"Odysseus will string the bow and shoot the arrow through the axes!" Cassandra crowed. "He will win Penelope and his kingdom back! And all of his enemies will be driven off."

As her words died away, there was dead silence for a few seconds. At last, when everyone realized that Odysseus's long troubled trip was finally at an end, a whoop of excitement went up. Everyone cheered and clapped for Athena's success.

Even Poseidon smiled gamely and shrugged. "My grade will still likely be an A. Who needs a plus, anyway?"

Athena gave Cassandra a huge hug. "I couldn't have done it without you," she said.

"Awesome!" said Homer as he rolled his notescroll tight. "After today's sold-out *Iliad* book event, my publisher is clamoring for my second book. And now that Odysseus is home safe and sound, I've got a complete draft! Of course I won't have time to edit what I've written. People are dying to read *The Odyssey*, and I want to give them what they want."

Athena looked really nervous to hear this. "But careful editing can help prevent mistakes," she began.

However, Homer was so wrapped up in his own excitement that he didn't seem to hear. Or maybe he did, because he looked at her and said, "And this time I'll mention you and your Trojan horse. Sorry about that omission in my first book."

Athena glanced at Cassandra. "You okay with that?" she asked.

Cassandra nodded. "It's history. I'm over it." And she was, mostly. It would always be a painful memory, as would the entire war, but she was tired of looking back and feeling unhappy. From now on she would look to the future! A future filled with new MOA and IM friends as well as her old friends from Troy, like Andromache.

"Well, I'm off," said Homer. "Don't want to miss my ride back to the IM with Hermes." He glanced at Cassandra. "See you in a few weeks?"

"Huh?" said Cassandra.

"Like I said, my publisher will want to bring *The Odyssey* out right way. And your mom has agreed to hold another event as soon as *The Odyssey* scrollbooks are in print. I'll want you at my side helping out. You're my good luck charm!"

"Really? Sure!" said Cassandra. How nice to be called lucky for a change!

Noticing how late it was getting, she looked at Athena. "Speaking of my mom, I'd better get home. It'll be dark soon, and I don't want her to worry."

"I'll take you in my chariot," Artemis volunteered.

"Want some company?" Apollo asked both girls.

Artemis shook her head, saying quickly, "No. My deer are kind of tired. I don't want too many riders weighing down the chariot."

The sun was setting as Cassandra and Artemis went out to the courtyard. Athena and Apollo followed them down the front steps of MOA to see them off. Artemis whistled, and two white golden-horned deer dashed from the forest nearby to hitch themselves to her chariot.

"I'm really sorry I couldn't reverse that curse," Apollo told Cassandra as they stood waiting for the chariot to be ready.

"You did your best," Athena reassured him.

Cassandra knew she was right. He'd made a real effort to undo the problem he'd caused her, and she didn't want him to feel bad.

"It's okay. I'm used to everyone thinking I'm a liar," she joked lamely. And indeed, only minutes after she'd made all those predictions back in the Hero-ology class-room, she'd heard others beginning to make comments that showed that no one credited her with being correct.

At least Apollo believed her, though. And maybe Athena. The goddessgirl seemed to be making a con-certed effort to dismiss her doubts, anyway.

"No, it's not okay," said Apollo. He stuck both hands into the pockets of his tunic, looking frustrated. "You're really nice, and you don't deserve to have people think-ing bad things about you. Hey, maybe I could bespell everyone to believe your prophecies no matter what."

"Put a spell on every single mortal *and* immortal?" Athena shook her head. "No, that wouldn't work."

"Well, I'm not giving up. I'm determined to reverse the cookie—I mean the curse," said Apollo.

Hearing this, Cassandra and Athena looked at each other, excitement slowly growing in their eyes.

"Reverse the cookies!" said Cassandra.

"The cookie fortunes, that is!" added Athena.

"That's it!" they said at the same time.

"*What's* it?" Apollo asked blankly.

"I don't get it either," Artemis told him.

As Artemis and Apollo looked on, the two girls outlined the brilliant plan they'd both come up with at the exact same moment.

"Cassandra can write fortunes that are the *opposite* of her true prophecies from now on—" Athena began, her blue-gray eyes sparkling.

"You're going to write predictions that are lies? On purpose?" Artemis asked.

Cassandra nodded. "But since people think I'm a liar, they'll believe the opposite of what I write. They'll believe the truth!" She looked at Apollo. "Think it'll work?"

He looked a little dizzy from their backward logic, but then he nodded. "It just might!"

Cassandra eyes went wide as she suddenly smelled peppermints again. A vision of a big white box appeared to her. Fancy writing on the label read:

Cassandra's Opposite Oracle-Os

"And we'll call my new cookies Opposite Oracle-Os!" she exclaimed.

"Mega-cool! How'd you think of that name so fast?" asked Apollo. "It's perfect." He high-fived her. Then they just stood there staring at each other. He really had amazing eyes, thought Cassandra. She kind of wished . . .

"Ahem!" Artemis cleared her throat. "Time to go. My deer are getting restless."

"Oh, yeah, sorry," said Cassandra. She stepped back from Apollo so she could climb inside the chariot with Artemis. Then she waved farewell to Athena and Apollo as the chariot lifted off. The two girls were silent as they whooshed upward, breaking through the clouds that were turning orange and pink from the setting sun.

When Artemis spoke at last, her words came as a total shock to Cassandra. "Don't play with my brother's feelings, okay? I mean, I can tell he likes you, and I just don't want you to pretend to like him too. In the end that'll only hurt him."

Apollo liked her? Cassandra's eyes bugged out. Did Artemis know what she was talking about? She was his sister, so maybe.

"He's been unlucky in love, or in *like* anyway," Artemis went on. "There was this girl, Daphne, who turned herself into a tree rather than hang out with him. And that's only the beginning. So I'm just saying—don't toy with his affections."

"I won't," Cassandra promised sincerely. At one time she might have, just to get back at him for the curse, but no longer.

After what Artemis had told her about Apollo being unlucky in love—er, *like*—Cassandra's heart went out to him. What was wrong with those other dumb girls who didn't like him? He seemed pretty cool to her. But then they had something big in common—telling fortunes!

She didn't like it when Agamemnon teased her, because his teasing seemed mean-spirited. But when Apollo joked with her, she could tell he meant it in fun. She *did* like him. But was Artemis right that he liked her back?

Once Artemis dropped her off in front of the Immortal Marketplace, Cassandra dashed into the bakery, feeling lighter than air from the excitement of visiting MOA. It was dark inside now that the IM was closed, but she saw a light in the back office and found her mom in there working on bookkeeping.

Cassandra perched on the edge of her mom's desk. Her dark eyes sparkled as she briefly explained what had happened and asked permission to try making the Opposite Oracle-Os. "And I promise I'll keep up with the rest of my bakery duties," she finished up. "So, pretty please with chocolate sprinkles on top?" Would her mom just tell her she wasn't allowed to make predictions, as usual? Cassandra held her breath, hoping for the best.

Hecuba thought for a moment, then a smile flashed across her face. "I think it's a terrific idea," she said. And since her mom had a pretty good feel for what would work and what wouldn't where sales were concerned, Cassandra took heart.

236

"Really? *Squee!*" Cassandra jumped up and did a little impromptu happy dance around the office. Then she went over to her mom's chair and gave her a hug.

"I predict that the new cookies are going to be a big success," said her mom.

"I predict you're right!" said Cassandra, which made them both laugh.

"And as far as your duties in the bakery," Hecuba said, "Andromache has asked to work here part-time."

Andromache! Cassandra could hardly wait to tell her all about what had happened at the Academy and about the Oracle-O's! She was glad she'd made friends with the kids at MOA, and that she'd see them again when they came to the Marketplace. But Andromache was someone who knew her past. Someone who really understood her. And she understood Andromache as well. She needed to tell her she wasn't mad at her for what had happened.

"I'm going to go find her," said Cassandra. "Back later!" She dashed to the door of the little office again, but then she paused in the doorway to look back at her mom.

"Know what? I think I've decided it's not so bad here," Cassandra admitted. "When we lived in Troy, I was a princess. I mean, I still am, but now I don't have to act like one. It was actually sort of tiresome to always have to be so proper about everything, you know? To go to fancy dinners and waste tons of time getting dressed for them. And back there, I had friends, but couldn't hang out with whoever I wanted to. Now I can choose my friends. It's cool."

"So are you saying you like living here in the IM? You want to stay?" her mom asked, a big smile filling her face.

"Yeah! I guess I am! And with Andromache working part-time in the bakery, I can work in the scrollbook shop mostly, right? I mean, except for when I'm doing fortunes for the new opposite cookie line or in school?"

"Sounds perfect!" said Hecuba. "I know Homer was very impressed with you as his assistant. And we'll invite other authors to hold events here soon too. You made me proud today, sweetie."

Cassandra grinned at her. Then came the sudden sharp, sweet smell of peppermints again.

As always, a vision followed. In it she saw Andromache and her, and a glossy white box. They were designing special packaging for the new line of Opposite Oracle-O cookies with her fortunes inside. Then she saw people lining up in the store to buy them. Tons of them. Awesome! She could hardly wait for this prophecy to come true!

"Well, I'm off to see Andromache," she told her mom. With a quick wave she dashed out the front door of the bakery and headed for Magical Wagical, happier than she'd been in a long while. Halfway down the Marketplace she did a lighthearted little skip and a twirl.

Just think! A godboy liked her, Homer and her mom thought she'd done well at the book signing, and she had a new job she liked in the bookshop. Not to mention a new line of fortune cookies coming up.

She was the *luckiest* girl in the whole Immortal Marketplace!

Epilogue

Athena

A FEW DAYS LATER HERMES' DELIVERY SERVICE dropped off a fancy white box at the Mount Olympus Academy cafeteria during breakfast. The box was labeled:

Cassandra's Opposite Oracle-Os

Oracle-O Bakery and Scrollbooks

Immortal Marketplace

Athena and her three goddessgirl friends were among the first to pick cookies out of the box. Or, rather, the cookies chose them. The right ones practically jumped into their hands.

"They're the newest thing and are flying off the shelves at the Oracle-O Bakery. The fortunes are all the opposite of what will actually happen," Pheme was saying to some girls as Athena and her friends went to their usual table.

"Wow! How mega-awesome is that?" Pandora responded to Pheme.

Soon MOA students were all buzzing with excitement about the new cookies. Each one contained a spoken fortune as usual, not written ones like the last Cassandra had sent.

"You will make an F minus today," Athena's cookie told her when she unwrapped it.

"Yay! An F minus is the opposite of an A plus," she said

happily. And as it turned out, Mr. Cyclops did give her an A plus on her Odysseus project first period. They'd been scored on three skills: manipulation, disasters, and quick saves. Apparently, she'd aced all three!

Aphrodite's cookie told her: "Your heart will get broken." And after school that day her crush, Ares, gave her a sweet gift of an unbroken heart charm on a necklace, just because.

Artemis's cookie announced: "You will miss every target you shoot at today." Which of course meant she didn't.

Persephone's said: "Your thumb will always be redder than any other student's at MOA." Since red was the color opposite to green on the color wheel, it meant her thumb would be green, as in she would always have the talent to grow the most beautiful flowers and plants of any student at the Academy.

Apollo was standing near their table when he opened his cookie. So all four goddessgirls heard it tell him: "You will not visit Cassandra at the IM."

"Well, I *am* going to the IM after school today so I can tell her how everyone likes the new cookies," he began. Then he glanced at Aphrodite, puzzled. "But is there some deeper meaning to this fortune that I'm not getting?" he asked her.

Since Aphrodite was the goddess of love, he must've figured she would know, Athena assumed.

Before Aphrodite could reply, Artemis rolled her eyes, and then sent him a teasing grin. "It means Cassandra likes you, dumbro. And she wants to hang out."

Apollo's eyes slowly widened with pleasure. "Really? Awesome!" he shouted, punching a fist in the air. "This is my *lucky* day!"

Don't miss the next adventure in
the Goddess Girls *series!*

Coming Spring 2014